DISNEY·PIXAR
MONSTERS, INC.
STORYBOOK COLLECTION

DISNEY PRESS
New York

TABLE OF CONTENTS

SUSTAINABLE FORESTRY INITIATIVE

Certified Sourcing
www.sfiprogram.org
SFI-00993
For Text Only

MONSTERS UNIVERSITY

Teaming Up

When Michael Wazowski was a young monster, he went on a field trip. His class visited Monsters, Inc., where the top Scarers in Monstropolis worked. These brave monsters went through special doors into the human world. They risked their lives to collect screams from dangerous human children. Then the screams were changed into energy for the town of Monstropolis.

Mike watched a Scarer open the door to a child's bedroom and followed, even though he wasn't supposed to. He stayed hidden as the Scarer made the child scream.

Afterward, Mike got into trouble for sneaking into the human world. But he didn't care. He'd decided he wanted to be a Scarer when he grew up. He'd go to school where the Scarer had gone—Monsters University.

Mike worked hard, studying and training, until he was accepted. On the first day of college, Mike's bus pulled up in front of the gates of a beautiful old campus.

"Wow," Mike breathed. He was finally at Monsters University! Mike checked out the clubs. There was an art club, an astronomy club, and something called the Scare Games, a contest in which students competed to see who was scariest.

On the first day of classes, Mike went to Scaring 101.

"Who can tell me the principles of an effective roar?" Professor Knight asked.

Mike started to answer. But just then—

"ROAAAAAR!" Another monster surprised everyone. "Good thing I didn't go all out, huh?" he said.

The monster who had roared was named James P. Sullivan. His friends called him Sulley. Scaring came easily to him, so he never studied. He was only interested in having fun.

Mike, on the other hand, studied every night. He didn't want to fail his final exam. If he did, he'd be out of the Scaring Program.

Mike and Sulley were not friends.

On the day of the final exam, Mike and Sulley began to argue. Then they got into a roaring face-off. They roared and snarled and growled. Soon everyone was watching, including the head of the School of Scaring, Dean Hardscrabble.

Sulley knocked over a scream can. It held the record-breaking scream Dean Hardscrabble had collected in her scaring days.

The canister hit the floor. *"Ahhhhhhhhhhhhhhhhhhh!"*

Hardscrabble's scream was gone.

Dean Hardscrabble decided to give Sulley and Mike their final exam.

Mike began a shadow approach with a crackle holler. He got ready to scream when Dean Hardscrabble stopped him. "I've seen enough."

Then it was Sulley's turn. He didn't wait to hear about the child he would scare. "ROOOOOOAAAAAR!"

Hardscrabble was not impressed. "This particular child is afraid of snakes. So a roar wouldn't make him scream, it would make him cry, alerting his parents, exposing the monster world, destroying life as we know it. I'm afraid I can't recommend that you continue in the Scaring Program."

She turned to Mike. "What you lack is something that can't be taught. You're not scary."

Mike was crushed. How would his dream of becoming a Scarer ever come true?

The next semester, Mike remembered the Scare Games. If he could prove to Dean Hardscrabble that he had what it took to be a great Scarer, maybe she would let him back into the program.

All he had to do was find a fraternity to join so he could compete.

There was only one option: Oozma Kappa, a group of misfits who weren't exactly scary.

But Dean Hardscrabble had made a deal with Mike. "If you win, I will let your entire team into the Scaring Program. But if you lose, you will leave Monsters University."

The problem was, Oozma Kappa needed one more member. "Anybody else want to join?" Mike asked the crowd who'd gathered for the games.

"The star player has just arrived," Sulley announced.

Mike was not happy. He and Sulley moved into the Oozma Kappa house and met Don, Art, Squishy, Terri, and Terry.

In the opening event in the Scare Games, the first team to make it through a tunnel of stinging glow urchins would win. The last would be out of the Scare Games.

"That as fast as you can go?" Mike asked Sulley.

"Just getting started," Sulley replied.

Mike and Sulley tied for second. But they'd left the rest of their team behind. Oozma Kappa came in last. Luckily another team was disqualified. Oozma Kappa was still in the games.

Sulley didn't think Oozma Kappa had a chance.

Oozma Kappa made it through the next challenge. But everyone except Mike and Sulley wanted to quit. The other teams were making fun of them. "We're built for other things," Don explained.

Mike decided to take the gang to Monsters, Inc. As they watched Scarers of all shapes and sizes, Mike realized something. "There's no one type of Scarer. The best Scarers use their differences to their advantage."

Mike and Sulley realized they'd been acting like jerks. "We could be a great team," Mike said. "We just need to start working together."

Oozma Kappa was more determined to win than ever. Mike trained them hard. They made it through the Don't Scare the Teen and the Hide and Sneak events. They were finally a team, and Mike was using all his scaring knowledge to lead them.

Sulley ran into Dean Hardscrabble. "Tomorrow each of you must prove you're undeniably scary." She pointed at Mike, who was out of earshot. "Do you think he is scary?"

Sulley was upset. Mike was smart, talented, and the hardest-working monster he'd ever met! But he was also small, friendly, and not exactly scary.

Suddenly, Sulley was worried. He really wanted his team to win—and tomorrow was the final Scare Games event.

The big day arrived. There were just two fraternities left: Roar Omega Roar and Oozma Kappa.

The monsters had to scare a robot child. One by one, the teams faced off. In the end, it came down to Mike.

"Roooooooooar!" Mike got a perfect score. Oozma Kappa had won the Scare Games!

Then Mike discovered that Sulley had cheated. He'd changed the settings to "easy" during Mike's turn. "You don't think I'm scary?"

"What was I supposed to do? Let the whole team fail?" Sulley replied.

Mike wanted to prove he *was* scary. He snuck through a door into the human world. He ended up in a camp cabin filled with dangerous children. But they didn't think he was scary either. Mike was really upset.

Sulley snuck through to get his teammate. But Mike wanted Sulley to leave. After what had happened, Mike didn't think he was special.

"I try to give people what they want, but all I do is let them

down," Sulley told Mike. "You're not the only failure here."

Mike was surprised. "How come you never told me that?"

"Because we weren't friends before," Sulley explained.

17

Mike realized they had to go back to the monster world. Suddenly camp rangers appeared. Mike and Sulley raced to the door they'd come through, but it wasn't active.

Mike and Sulley teamed up to frighten the rangers. They clawed the floor, slammed the door, and toppled the bunk beds. Then Sulley roared. It was such a big roar that the rangers' screams created enough energy to make the door come back on.

Mike and Sulley made it back to Monsters University. But they were kicked out of the school. Luckily their teammates got to stay.

Mike and Sulley made a great team.

Before long they'd gotten their first jobs at Monsters, Inc. They hoped one day they could work on a scare floor. . . .

Disney·PIXAR
MONSTERS, INC.
Parade Day Dash

Mike Wazowski crumpled up the last piece of crepe paper and stepped back to take a look at his work.

"That's it!" he said to his best friend, Sulley. "It's perfect!"

Sulley hopped up on the parade float they'd been building all day. It was decorated with balloons and streamers, and had a row of doors in the middle, just like on the Scare Floor.

It was the best float Sulley had ever seen. And when he rode it tomorrow, he'd be doing his favorite thing—pretending to scare!

Sulley crept behind one of the doors and threw it open. *"Rrraaargh!"* he roared.

Mike put on his best announcer voice: "Introducing the Grand Monster of this year's Monstropolis Day parade . . . Mr. James P. Sullivan!"

Every year, Monsters, Inc. held a big parade on the day Monstropolis had been discovered. Since Sulley had collected more screams than any other Scarer that year, including Randall, he had been asked to lead the parade. It was a huge honor!

"You're ready to go," Mike said. "Tomorrow, we'll hook up my car to the float, and you'll lead the entire parade. All the little monsters will love seeing you pretend to scare." He smiled at his friend. "I think you're going to be the best Grand Monster this town's ever seen."

Sulley grinned. "Want to take a practice drive along the parade route?"

"Sure. Hop in!" Mike exclaimed. He and Sulley rode along.

The sun was setting. It was a beautiful night in Monstropolis. Main Street was already lined with flags, banners, and even sour-lemonade stands.

As he and Mike passed the grandstand, Sulley could see where he would give the signal to start the fireworks at the end of the parade.

Then Mike noticed something strange. Someone was moving behind the grandstand!

When they'd finished driving along the parade route, Mike drove back to Monsters, Inc. They left Mike's car with the float and walked home. They wanted to be sure to get a good night's sleep.

The next afternoon, Sulley put on his tall Grand Monster hat. Mike gave him a thumbs-up. He looked perfect! Then the friends hurried off to Monsters, Inc.

In the parking lot, everyone was getting ready for the parade. Some monsters set up floats while others carried balloons. A tall monster wearing a band uniform waved her tentacles in the air. "Has anybody seen my flute?" she cried.

Mike used a hook to attach his car to Sulley's float. "She's ready to go!" He smiled.

Sulley jumped up onto the float. But when Mike put the key in the ignition, his car wouldn't start!

"Of all days," Mike muttered, opening the hood.

As Mike checked the engine, Sulley anxiously watched the other monsters start to pull their floats out of the parking lot.

Crowds of people were already lining the streets. The parade would be starting soon.

"Everything okay over here?" asked Mr. Waternoose, the head of Monsters, Inc. "We need you at the head of the parade, Sulley."

Sulley explained that the car wasn't working. Just then, Randall came up, almost as if he'd been waiting. "My float is working perfectly," he said to Mr. Waternoose. "Perhaps I should lead the parade?"

Mr. Waternoose sighed. "I suppose that would be best. Sorry, Sulley. I'm sure you understand."

Randall's float was covered in mirrors, all reflecting his sneaky image. "Sorry about your float, Sulley," he hissed. "Let me know if you need a lift to the gas station."

That's when Sulley noticed a puddle on the ground next to Mike's car. He sniffed it. "It's gas," he said.

Mike bent down to look, and he gasped. "I can't believe I missed this. It's Randall's footprint! He emptied the tank on purpose. That sneaky reptile!"

"We can't let him get away with this!" Sulley exclaimed.

"We *won't* let him get away with this!" Mike replied. "We have to fill the tank and catch that parade!"

It took Mike and Sulley a while to get more fuel, but before long, they were racing out of Monsters, Inc. Mike steered the float alongside a marching band at the end of the parade.

"Pardon us," Sulley called. "Coming through!"

Mike honked his horn to the same beat as the giant tuba, and Sulley tipped his hat to the conductor.

"Go get 'em, Sulley!" the band cried.

The Monstropolis Day parade was known for its giant balloons shaped like famous monsters. They hovered over the street, held down by strong ropes to keep them from flying away.

The crowd cheered as Mike drove Sulley's float under a balloon in the shape of Mr. Waternoose. He gave the crowd a thumbs-up, then sped on.

Meanwhile, Sulley showed off some of his best scaring. He jumped out of different doors on the float and roared. The crowd clapped and whistled!

Mike squeezed past a float with Monster Scouts tossing gummy worms and grasshopper cookies to the crowd. The Monster Scouts squealed with delight when Sulley jumped out from one of the doors, pretending to scare them. Suddenly, Sulley had an idea.

"Mike," he called down. "When you see Randall, pull up alongside his float. I have an idea that will knock his socks off."

They could see Randall now, blowing kisses to the crowd at the front of the parade. Mike wove through a line of monster-cycle riders until the float was next to Randall's float.

"So glad you could make it after all!" Randall cackled to Mike. "Too bad you missed all the fun."

But then Sulley burst out from behind one of the doors on his float and gave Randall the scare of his life. *"RRRAAARRGH!"* Sulley roared.

Randall was startled, but the crowd cheered and clapped. They thought it was part of the show!

"That was awesome!" a boy monster called to Sulley as Mike drove them to the front of the parade. Sulley winked and tossed the boy his Grand Monster hat.

The crowd cheered. No Grand Monster had ever done that.

Along the way, Sulley waved to the crowd. Then he pretended to scare them, and they cheered. Sulley loved seeing everyone have such a good time! Being a Grand Monster was more fun than he had imagined.

When they reached the end of the route, Sulley climbed to the top of the grandstand. There were monsters as far as he could see. Together with the rest of the crowd, he cheered as each float passed by—even Randall's.

As the sun began to set, Sulley went to the microphone.

"We hope you enjoyed the Monstropolis Day parade!" His voice echoed over the crowd. Everyone cheered. Then he announced, "Let the fireworks begin!"

Boom! Sparkling lights exploded in the sky, lighting up the entire town center. As everyone "ooohed" and "ahhed," Sulley smiled at Mike. "Thanks, pal," he said. "You sure saved the day." Mike gave him a thumbs-up. "Hey, what are friends for?"

MONSTERS, INC.

Welcome to Monsters, Inc.

Every night, all around the world, monsters called Scarers would sneak through children's closet doors. It was their job to collect screams. Those screams powered the city of Monstropolis, where all the monsters lived.

One night, a little boy woke up. A monster was standing in his bedroom.

"*Ahh!*" screamed the boy.

"*Ahh!*" screamed the monster.

Suddenly, the lights came on. It was just a pretend bedroom and a robotic boy. The monster was actually in a training classroom at the biggest power company in Monstropolis: Monsters, Inc.

The teacher sighed. The monster had left the closet door open. Again.

"Leaving the door open is the worst mistake any employee can make, because . . . ?" the teacher asked.

"It could let in a draft?" the monster guessed.

"It could let in a child!" a voice boomed. Mr. Waternoose, the president of Monsters, Inc., stormed in. He was responsible for making sure his Scarers were trained to collect enough screams to power Monstropolis. But everyone knew that if a human child came into Monstropolis, it would be very dangerous.

"There's nothing more toxic or deadly than a human child," Mr. Waternoose exclaimed.

Unlike the Scarers-in-training, one monster was very good at collecting screams. His name was James P. Sullivan—"Sulley" for short. He was a big, furry blue monster, and one of Monstropolis's top Scarers.

Across town, Sulley exercised in his apartment. He had to stay in top shape if he wanted to keep being scary. His roommate and best friend, Mike Wazowski, coached him. "Feel the burn!" Mike ordered as Sulley pushed heavy furniture across the room.

Sulley was famous for collecting more screams than any other employee at Monsters, Inc., which made him very important. Human children were getting harder to scare. Sulley was one of the only monsters who could still frighten them.

One day, a coworker named Randall watched Mike and Sulley getting ready for work. Randall was a mean monster who could blend into walls. He was very jealous of Sulley. He would do anything to be the top Scarer.

Randall jumped out and startled Mike. "I'm in the zone today," he sneered. "Going to be doing some serious scaring. Putting up some big numbers."

When their shift started, all the monsters went to the Scare Floor. A long conveyor belt dropped a child's closet door at each monster's station.

When a red signal flashed, each Scarer would walk through his door and into the room of a sleeping human child. If all went well, the child would scream, filling up a power canister.

Sulley glanced at the scare scoreboard. He and Randall had almost the same score. "May the best monster win." Sulley held out his hand to Randall.

"I plan to," Randall replied.

A buzzer went off. It was time to scare! Randall quickly made a lot of children scream. But Sulley frightened an entire slumber party! Mike popped in a fresh canister each time one filled up to collect as many of the screams as possible. Sulley was back in the lead.

Suddenly, a warning alarm sounded. A Scarer named George Sanderson had returned from the human world with a child's sock on his back! All the monsters gasped. A child's sock could be just as toxic as a child!

In seconds, a squad from the Child Detection Agency arrived to decontaminate George.

As soon as work ended, Mike rushed to meet his girlfriend, Celia. She also worked at Monsters, Inc. Celia was a pretty monster with one eye and snakes for hair. Mike had planned a special date for her birthday.

But Roz, the cranky office manager, blocked Mike's way. "Fun-filled evening planned for tonight?" she asked.

"Well, as a matter of fact—" Mike began.

"Then I'm sure you filed your paperwork," Roz said.

Mike gulped. He'd forgotten to do it—again!

Luckily, Sulley offered to do it for him.

When Sulley returned to the Scare Floor, he noticed a closet door that had been left behind.

"Hello?" Sulley called out.

No one answered. Sulley opened the door to take a peek. But the room was empty.

Sulley shrugged and closed the door. Just then, he heard a noise. He turned around and saw a little girl grabbing his tail!

"Ahhh!" Sulley screamed. He tried to run, but the little girl thought it was a game.

No matter how hard Sulley tried, he couldn't get the little girl to go back through her closet door. He decided to find Mike—he'd know what to do!

Sulley hid the little girl and left Monsters, Inc. with her. He raced to the restaurant where Mike was having dinner with Celia.

Sulley peered in and saw Mike. He raced inside and squeezed into a booth next to Mike. He held up a menu so Celia couldn't hear him. "Look in the bag," he whispered to Mike.

"What bag?" Mike asked.

Sulley looked down and his jaw dropped. The bag—and the child—were walking away!

The little girl hopped up on a table.

"Boo!" she said with a giggle.

The monsters nearby panicked. The chef called the Child Detection Agency. "There's a kid here! A human kid!" he yelled into the phone.

The little girl giggled as she ran around the restaurant. Mike found an empty box and scooped her up into it. He tossed the box to Sulley.

"Let's get out of here!" Mike shouted.

Just as they escaped, the CDA arrived. They started to decontaminate monsters. Celia and Mike were separated from each other.

Mike wanted to go back to help, but Sulley grabbed him. They needed to run!

Sulley and Mike brought the child to their apartment. They put on oven mitts and flippers so she couldn't touch them.

Outside their window, CDA helicopters flew by. The CDA officers were searching the city for the child.

Mike and Sulley knew they had to keep her hidden or they would be in big trouble.

But the child wouldn't keep still!

She chased Mike around the apartment. As he tried to get away, Mike tripped into a trash can.

The little girl giggled. Her laughter made the lights burn so bright, they popped!

"What was that?" asked Sulley.

"I have no idea," Mike replied, shocked.

They gave the little girl paper and crayons to color with while they tried to figure out how to get her back home. Somehow, they needed to get to her closet door.

Soon the little girl rubbed her eyes and yawned. Sulley laid down some newspaper on the floor for her to sleep on. But the little girl hopped right into his bed.

"Hey, you're going to get your germs all over it!" Sulley exclaimed.

The girl just snuggled under the covers. Sulley sighed. He knew it was no use.

He was about to leave when the little girl pointed to his closet door fearfully. She held up a picture she had drawn.

"Hey, that looks like Randall," Sulley said. "Randall must be your monster." He realized the little girl was afraid Randall would come through the closet door and scare her.

Sulley tried to show her that there was nothing in his closet. Finally, he agreed to stay with her until she fell asleep. As he watched her drift off, Sulley couldn't help thinking she didn't look so dangerous after all.

Sulley told Mike he wanted to bring the girl back to Monsters, Inc. so they could find her closet door and get her home. He had even thought of a name for her: Boo.

Mike didn't agree. "What are we going to do, waltz right up to the factory?" he asked.

That gave Sulley an idea. If he and Mike made Boo look like a monster, then they *could* take her right into the factory!

The next morning, that's just what they did.

Now all they had to do was get her home. . . .

Disney · PIXAR
MONSTERS, INC.
Sulley to the Rescue

Mike and Sulley were two monsters with one giant problem: they had accidentally let a human child into Monstropolis! All monsters believed that human kids were toxic.

It was up to Sulley and Mike to get the little girl named Boo back to the human world before anyone found her. In order to do that, they needed to get to her closet door at Monsters, Inc.

Sulley dressed Boo up as a monster, and the friends headed to the factory. Just as they got there, a mean monster named Randall and his assistant, Fungus, nearly spotted them. Sulley, Mike, and Boo hid in a bathroom stall.

Fungus showed Randall the front page of the morning newspaper. "It's the kid you were after!" he cried.

"Will you be quiet?" Randall exclaimed. "I'll take care of the kid."

Sulley realized that Boo was in danger. They needed to get her home quickly.

While Mike and Sulley searched for her closet door, Boo wandered off! The two friends split up to find her.

Unfortunately, Randall found Mike first. He'd figured out that Mike and Sulley had the child.

"Where's the kid?" demanded Randall. When Mike wouldn't tell him, Randall said he'd bring the kid's door to the Scare Floor at lunchtime. He promised that if Mike and Sulley brought the child, she could go home and none of them would get in trouble.

Just as Sulley found Boo, Mike ran up to him. "I found us a way out of this mess," he exclaimed. "Come on!" He led the way to the Scare Floor, where Boo's door was waiting. "There it is, just like Randall said!" he cried.

"Randall?" Sulley asked. "We can't trust Randall. He's after Boo."

But Mike was sure everything was fine. To prove it, he opened the door to Boo's room and went inside.

He climbed on her bed.

Suddenly, a box came down over Mike. It was a trap!

Sulley and Boo hid while Randall wheeled the box away on a cart. Then they followed Randall through the factory and down a long, dark hallway to a hidden workshop.

Randall let out an evil laugh as he opened the box. When he found Mike instead of the girl, he was angry. But that didn't stop him from following his wicked plan.

"I'm about to revolutionize the scaring industry," Randall said. "And when I do, even the great James P. Sullivan is going to be working for me!"

Randall had invented a machine that could suck the screams out of children. And he was going to test it on Mike!

Luckily, Sulley pulled the machine's plug out of the wall and saved Mike. The three friends ran for their lives.

"Follow me!" Sulley called to Mike. "I have an idea." Sulley decided they needed to find Mr. Waternoose, president of Monsters, Inc., and tell him what was going on.

When they found Mr. Waternoose, Mike explained Randall's evil plan.

"I'm sorry you got mixed up in this," Mr. Waternoose said with a heavy sigh.

A closet door landed behind them, and Mike turned around. "Uh, sir? That's not her door," Mike said slowly.

"I know," Mr. Waternoose said. Randall suddenly appeared beside him. "It's yours."

Mr. Waternoose grabbed Boo and pushed Mike and Sulley through the door and into the Himalayan mountains—in the human world!

Mike was furious. "What a great idea!" he shouted at Sulley. "Going to your old pal, Waternoose. Too bad he was in on the whole thing!"

Sulley could only think about one thing: Boo. He had to get back and save her. She was in serious trouble!

Mike was too angry to help, so Sulley went alone. Using a sled, he raced through the snow to a local village to find a child's closet door that could lead him back to Monsters, Inc.

When he got back, Sulley rushed to Randall's secret lab. He destroyed the machine and rescued Boo!

As Sulley dashed away with Boo, Mike suddenly arrived to help. He had changed his mind.

"I'm glad you came back, Mike," Sulley said.

Mike smiled. "Someone's got to take care of you, you big hairball."

They ran all over Monsters, Inc., looking for a way out as Randall chased after them.

The friends dashed to the Scare Floor and jumped onto a conveyor belt. Mike and Sulley had discovered that a human child's laughter was even more powerful than screams. So Mike made Boo laugh to power the machine. They needed to get to Boo's door before Randall could catch them.

Mike and Sulley jumped in and out of closets trying to lose Randall and find Boo's door.

Suddenly, Randall got close enough to grab Boo!

Sulley fought the evil monster off, but he lost his balance and clung to the edge of a closet door.

Boo knew she had to help Sulley. She hopped on Randall's back and fought him, too!

"She's not scared of you anymore," Sulley said as he climbed up from the edge.

Working together, Sulley and Boo shoved Randall through a door to the human world.

The door fell to the ground and it shattered. They had actually beaten him!

Boo was so proud.

"That's right, Boo. You did it!" Sulley told her.

But the friends weren't safe yet.

Mr. Waternoose and the Child Detection Agency were now controlling the power and the doors. Mike, Sulley, and Boo jumped down from the conveyor belt to the Scare Floor. They landed behind Boo's door.

"This is the CDA," said one of the agents. "Come out slowly with the child in plain sight."

Mike took Boo's monster costume and ran off. The CDA chased after him, and Sulley and Boo could escape. Unfortunately, Mr. Waternoose spotted them. "Give me the child!" he yelled.

Mr. Waternoose chased Sulley and Boo into a child's bedroom.

"Just leave her alone!" Sulley demanded.

"I can't," Mr. Waternoose said. "Scaring isn't enough anymore. I'll kidnap a thousand children before I let this company die!"

Suddenly, the lights came on. The bedroom was actually a training room—and Mike and the CDA had seen the whole thing!

It turned out the CDA had been keeping a close eye on Mr. Waternoose all along. Now they had the evidence they needed to prove he was trying to kidnap children. Mr. Waternoose was arrested by the head of the CDA—who was actually Roz, the cranky Monsters, Inc. office manager!

It was finally time for Boo to go home. Roz told Sulley that once he took her back to her room, he couldn't see her again. Her door would be shredded so it couldn't be used for scaring anymore.

"Good-bye, Boo," Sulley said sadly as he tucked her into bed. Then he walked back into Monsters, Inc.

Mike tried to cheer him up. "We got Boo home. Hey, at least we had some laughs."

Suddenly, Sulley's face brightened. Mike had just given him an excellent idea!

Before long, Monsters, Inc. had changed completely. Sulley had become the president. And since Boo had shown him that laughter was ten times more powerful than screams, the Scare Floor became a Laugh Floor! Monsters told jokes and did silly tricks to collect laughter from children. It was a huge success, and Monstropolis had more energy than ever!

Sulley missed Boo, though. He still had a tiny piece of her door taped to his clipboard.

Then, one day, Mike had a surprise for Sulley.

"Ta-da!" said Mike.

Sulley gasped.

Mike had put Boo's door back together! Now Sulley could visit Boo whenever he liked.

Sulley opened the door. "Boo?"

"Kitty!" replied Boo, using her special nickname for Sulley.

The two friends were back together at last.

MONSTERS, INC.

Funny Business

The streets of Monstropolis were filled with monsters on their way to work. It was slow going as Mike and Sulley headed to Monsters, Inc. They had to stop every few feet to shake someone's paw, claw, or tail.

"You guys are amazing," a monster named Needleman called.

"Yeah, you're really lighting up Monstropolis," his friend Smitty added.

"That's our job!" Mike waved proudly.

"Sorry we can't stay and chat," Sulley said. "Got to get to work!"

Things had changed at the factory since Mike and Sulley had discovered that kids' laughter generated more energy than their screams.

Mike had become one of the best Laugh Collectors on the floor. And Sulley was the president of the factory now. There was always a lot of work to do!

In Sulley's office, a mountain of paperwork was stacked on the desk. Sulley pressed the message button on his phone. "You have thirty . . . new . . . messages," it said.

"It was hard enough filling out paperwork for screams," Mike said with a sigh. "But now, I'm getting so many laughs, my paperwork has tripled. And you, Mr. Big Shot Factory President, have *everyone's* paperwork to worry about."

Sulley nodded. "I can't believe I'm saying this, but I actually miss Roz. She really kept everything in order."

"You miss Roz, huh?" a low, growly voice said from the doorway. Mike and Sulley jumped.

"I'd know that voice anywhere," Mike whispered. It could only belong to the monster they'd just been talking about.

Before Monsters, Inc. had become a laugh factory, Roz was the office manager. She was strict and had always hounded Mike for his paperwork. But in reality, she had been working undercover. So one day she'd left, and she hadn't been back. Until now . . .

"Roz?" the friends asked.

"Guess again," said the voice.

The monster sounded like Roz. She looked like Roz. Only she wasn't Roz. "The name's Floz," the monster growled. "I'm the new office manager."

"New office manager?" Sulley said in surprise. He cleared his throat. "Uh, nice to meet you. I'm—"

"I know who you are," Floz interrupted. "My cousin told me all about you two."

"You're Roz's cousin!" Mike exclaimed, his eye wide.

"She especially told me about you, Wazowski," Floz said.

Mike glanced at Sulley. That didn't sound good.

Floz handed them a pile of paperwork. "These new forms need to be filled out by noon today."

"What?" Sulley sputtered. "But I haven't even finished the *old* forms."

"Don't worry, Sulley," Mike said later as they headed to the Laugh Floor. "Floz can't be any worse than Roz, can she? Besides, maybe she'll help keep things in order, just like you said!"

Mike and Sulley spent the morning working. Before they knew it, it was lunchtime. They went to the cafeteria.

"Mmm, try the burnt-onion burrito," Sulley suggested.

"Sure," Mike said. "Maybe after I—"

"Fill out these forms?" Floz slid over to their table. She dropped a stack of papers in front of Mike, knocking over his glass. Chocolate milk soaked the forms.

"That does it, Wazowski," Floz growled. "Good thing I have extra copies right here."

"Well, wouldn't you know it, my pen is in my locker!" Mike jumped up, pulling Sulley after him. When they got to the locker room, Mike grabbed an extra sandwich from his bag. "Whew," he said, sighing.

But before he could take a bite, Needleman and Smitty came in. Needleman was carrying a giant binder. "Floz told us to give you this," Smitty said.

Sulley peeked inside. "There must be fifty forms in here! And it's still our break! What are we going to do, Mike?"

"I know what I'm *not* going to do," Mike said, taking his bag and leading Sulley to the lobby. "I officially declare today NO MORE PAPERWORK DAY. Come on. Let's take a walk."

They pushed open the front door—and there stood Floz. "Not so fast, boys. I forgot to give you the forms where you explain why you're late handing in your forms."

"Run for it, Sulley!" cried Mike. "If she can't catch us, she can't give us more paperwork!"

The guys sped down the hall. Floz stayed with them every step of the way. "We'll have to hide," Sulley huffed.

They ducked into a supply room and squeezed behind a dusty old filing cabinet. But Floz spotted them!

"We were just searching for more forms," Mike said quickly. He opened a creaky file drawer and pulled out a cobweb. "Guess this will go under C."

They raced out of the room with Floz close behind.

Mike and Sulley dove into a trash can.

"I smell unfinished paperwork." Floz sniffed them out. She
yanked off the lid of the trash can.

"Let's go, buddy!" Sulley cried. He and Mike scrambled out
of the trash, escaping just in time.

"In here!" Sulley cried. A closet door was just sliding into place on the Laugh Floor. They slipped inside.

A boy sat up in bed and stared.

"Whew! That was close!" Mike said.

"How's this for close?" Floz stuck her head between the friends.

"Floz!" they gasped.

"Monsters?" the boy asked from his bed.

Floz suddenly turned pale. "It's a . . . a child!" she stammered.

"This must be your first time with a real child," Sulley said, realizing what was wrong. "Don't be afraid. They're harmless."

But Floz backed away. *Squeak!* She had stepped on a toy ducky.

"Ahhhh!" Floz cried.

The boy started to look frightened. Then his puppy ran in and tried to lick Floz. *"Ahhhhh!"* she screamed louder.

The boy clutched his blanket. "Scary monsters!" he cried.

"Mike! Do something!" exclaimed Sulley.

"What should I do?" Mike asked. "The only way Floz would be funny is if . . . oh, wait, I know!" He reached into his bag and pulled out a pie topped with whipped cream. "Hey, Floz! Catch!" he yelled.

Mike tossed the pie at Floz. *Splat!* A direct hit! The pie slowly slid down her face. She was covered in whipped cream.

Floz blinked and licked her lips.

The boy laughed. "More!" he cried.

"Sorry, kid," said Mike. "Only one pie per customer."

The three monsters backed out of the room. On the other side of the door, Mike and Sulley grinned at Floz.

"You're a natural!" Mike said. "You might have a future on the Laugh Floor."

Floz nodded slowly. "That was quick thinking in there, Wazowski," she grumbled.

"You see?" Mike smiled. "It takes more than paperwork to run a funny business."

"So, Floz," Sulley said. "It's okay if we skip some of those forms, seeing how busy we are collecting laughs. Right?"

"Not a chance," Floz growled.

Mike and Sulley groaned.

"But I suppose the deadlines can be extended," she said. "A little." She paused. "Oh, and Wazowksi," Floz said, "*never* throw a pie in my face again."

"Yes, Floz," they answered. At least with Floz around, things would be in order again. Sort of.

Disney·PIXAR
MONSTERS, INC.
Dayscare

"**G**ood morning, President Sullivan," Celia said as Sulley walked through the front doors of Monsters, Inc.

"Good morning, Celia," he said with a wave. "You know you don't need to call me that."

Celia giggled. She was just teasing him. She knew he was the same old Sulley, even though he was now head of Monsters, Inc. But it was a big change from his days as Top Scarer.

Sulley had just settled in behind his desk when his assistant buzzed him.

"Good morning, President Sullivan," he said. "Your ten o'clock Joke Brainstorming meeting has been pushed back to eleven. The Canister Safety Committee will now meet at nine thirty. And your weekly Laugh Training Seminar will be at two o'clock."

"Thank you," Sulley said, sighing. He loved his new job, but sometimes there were just too many boring meetings!

Just then, his phone rang. It was the head of Monster Resources. "I'm sorry, President Sullivan," she said, "but both daycare teachers are out today with Swampy Pox!"

Hmmm, Sulley thought, it must be fun teaching all those little monsters. Suddenly, he had an idea—a crazy idea.

"Clear my schedule!" he called to his assistant. "I'll take care of this," he said into the phone. He headed to the Laugh Floor to find Mike.

"Sulley!" Mike said happily when he saw his friend. "Guess who just filled his daily laugh quota?"

"Perfect!" Sulley smiled. "That means you can teach daycare with me today!"

Mike's eye grew wide. "Um . . . laughs are one thing. I'm not sure about teaching an entire class of little monsters . . ."

But Sulley grabbed his best friend and dragged him to the daycare room.

The head of Monster Resources looked very pleased to see them.

"Look everyone!" she cried. "It's your substitute daycare teachers, Mr. James P. Sullivan and Mr. Mike Wazowski! Guys, meet Fungus Jr., Patrick, Martha, Pearl, Gretel, and Randall's nephew, Rex."

She smiled. "See ya!" Then she ran out the door.

"Cute kids," said Sulley. He wondered why the head of Monster Resources was in such a rush. "She must have a meeting to get to," he said. "Well, no meetings for me—today is all about fun!"

"Hello, everyone!" Sulley said to the class. "We're going to have such a good time today—"

In the middle of his speech, all the little monsters jumped up and started going wild.

"Ouch!" said Mike as he got hit with a stuffed monster. He shook his head at Sulley. "Fun, huh?" he said sarcastically. "Well, what are we supposed to do now, Mr. President?"

"Um . . . play a game?" Sulley suggested.

"All right," said Mike. "How about hide-and-shriek?"

"Mike," said Sulley. "It's called hide-and-seek now, remember?"

"Whatever," said Mike. "Okay kids, who wants to play . . ."

"*Ahhhh!*" the kids screamed and ran off to hide. Mike shrugged at Sulley. "Guess they like this game." He covered his eye and began to count. "Ready or not, here I come!"

One by one, Mike and Sulley found the kids. Then Sulley quickly counted them. "Um, Mike, I think we're missing one," he said.

"You're right," said Mike. "Randall's nephew, Rex."

"And you'll never find him," said Gretel. The rest of the little monsters started giggling.

"This is why our teachers never let us play hide-and-seek anymore," said Fungus Jr.

Mike gulped. "Sulley, I don't like this one bit!"

Just then Sulley had an idea. "It's too bad we can't find Rex," he said loudly. "Because it's snack time!"

"Here I am!" said Rex, suddenly reappearing behind Mike.

"We want snacks! We want snacks!" all of the little monsters chanted.

Mike ran to the cupboard and began handing out treats he thought the kids would like—gummy bugs, rotten apples, and mud-covered sardines.

Sulley smiled. "See Mike, all we needed to do was . . ."

"FOOD FIGHT!" the kids screamed. Instantly, food started flying across the room. Gummy bugs stuck to the walls and Sulley's fur. Mike got splattered with a handful of mud-covered sardines.

Little Martha crawled under the snack table and watched as she munched on a rotten apple.

"What a mess!" Mike moaned. Once he and Sulley had gotten the place cleaned up, they looked at each other. What should they do next?

"Maybe something quiet," Mike suggested.

"Let's try toy time," said Sulley.

Though it seemed like a good idea at first, it didn't last long.

"Mine!" Martha screeched.

"No, mine!" Pearl wailed.

Mike and Sulley tried everything to calm down the kids. They found toys in the closet. They played more games. But they just couldn't get the kids to settle down.

"Tie my shoes, Mike Wazowski!" Fungus Jr. demanded.

Mike rolled his eye. "You have got to be kidding me. A little help here!" he cried to Sulley.

"Right back at ya!" Sulley called back.

The day kept getting worse. Finger painting was a catastrophe. So was a game of jump rope. Even dress up was a nightmare.

"Is this day over yet?" asked Mike.

Sulley checked the clock. "Not even close," he said.

"This is a total disaster," Mike groaned.

"There's got to be something we haven't tried," replied Sulley.

"You know, I just don't think so," Mike said, frustrated. "I think we've literally tried everything!"

"I'm sure there must be something . . ." said Sulley.

"I'm sure there must be something." Mike imitated Sulley's voice, acting like a kid.

"Don't be mean," Sulley said.

"Don't be mean." Mike imitated him again.

"Mike," Sulley said.

"Mike," Mike repeated.

"No, Mike—look!" Sulley pointed to the monster kids, who sat on the floor, quietly watching them.

The kids burst into applause.

"Again! Again!" Pearl cried. "We like your play!"

Now that they had the kids' attention, Mike and Sulley realized what they should do: put on a puppet show!

Mike told tons of jokes. And Sulley did lots of scary voices. The kids laughed and laughed. They had lunch, then they took a long nap.

Finally, it was time for all the little monsters to go home.

Once everyone had been picked up, the two friends looked at each other and chuckled. Mike was covered with paint, and Sulley had a lollipop stuck to his fur.

"That was the toughest day I think I've ever had," Sulley said with a loud yawn. "I guess it's time to go home."

Mike eyed the pile of nap rugs in the corner. "Hey, let's rest for a minute before we head home," he suggested.

"Good idea," said Sulley. "Hey, these are pretty comfortable!"

The next morning, Patrick was the first student to arrive.

"Oh, look!" Patrick's mom said to him. "Mr. Sullivan and Mr. Wazowski are already here. They must have had such a great time yesterday they didn't want to miss a minute of today!"

Mike and Sulley sat up groggily. They had been so tired they'd slept all night! They looked at each other, and then at Patrick, who was smiling.

It was going to be a long day.

Disney·PIXAR
MONSTERS, INC.
A Monster of a Meal

SCARE THE COOK!

"Just a pinch of oregano," Sulley muttered to himself. He sprinkled some seasoning into the bubbling mixture he was cooking. Then he slurped a spoonful. Not bad, but something was still missing.

Sulley grabbed a can labeled FISH GUTS EXTRA STINKY from the shelf. He added exactly one teaspoon. Then he tasted the stew again. It was perfect.

Sulley poured the mixture into a pie dish, laid a crust over the top, and put the whole thing in the oven. Grandma Sulley's secret recipe for vegetable rot pie was sure to take the prize at the annual Monstropolis Cook-Off the next weekend. But Sulley was making a practice pie first, just in case.

Every year, the winning recipe in the cook-off was printed in *Stomach Churner* magazine. Sulley was determined to win this year using one of his grandmonster's recipes. He knew she would be very proud if he won.

But when the pie was done baking, Sulley wasn't sure it would win. The fish guts weren't stinky enough. The vegetables weren't slimy enough. His rot pie just wasn't as good as Grandma Sulley's.

"Maybe I should make something else," Sulley said. He looked through his grandmonster's recipes.

"I know! I'll make chilly chili. That will definitely wow the judges!" he exclaimed. Chilly chili was ice cream made from three-bean chili with extra onions. Grandma Sulley's secret ingredients were cherries and sauerkraut on top.

Sulley hurried off to the grocery store to buy the ingredients. When he got there, he saw his best friend, Mike Wazowski, out front.

"Mike! Fancy running into you here," Sulley said. "What are you shopping for?"

"Oh, I'm just getting ready to bake a little something called . . . cabbage cake!" Mike said. He juggled three stinky cabbages in the air. "No monster can resist it! I know it'll win the first prize in the cook-off."

"Well, may the best cook win," Sulley said. But as he walked away, he was feeling a little nervous. Mike's cabbage cake was famous. Maybe chilly chili wasn't good enough.

I could make smelly-socks soufflé instead, Sulley thought. He began gathering ingredients, when . . .

"Hey, Sulley!"

This time it was Celia, Mike's girlfriend. Her shopping cart was almost full.

"Are you shopping for the cook-off?" she asked. "I am, too! What are you making?"

"Well, I—" Sulley started.

"I'm making sewer-sludge s'mores!" Celia exclaimed. She was so excited, she didn't even wait to hear what Sulley was making. "And I just know I'm going to win!"

"Okay," Sulley said as Celia hurried away, her snakes hissing happily. "Good luck, I guess."

Wow, Sulley thought. Mike's and Celia's dishes sounded delicious. Maybe smelly-socks soufflé wasn't going to be good enough, either. He thought hard. What would Grandma Sulley do?

"I've got to think big," Sulley said. "I have to make something really special. Whether it's an appetizer, an entrée, or a dessert. Or, maybe . . . yes, that's it!"

Sulley began throwing ingredients into his basket. Curdled milk. Broccoli. Pickled herring. Then he raced home excitedly.

One week later, the Monstropolis town square was packed with monsters for the cook-off. Tables lined the sidewalks, covered with different types of food. Some monsters had made main courses, like sauerkraut chowder. Others had made desserts, like Mike's cabbage cake. Even George Sanderson, from Monsters, Inc., was there. He had made slimeburgers.

"What did you make, Sulley?" Mike asked. He tried to peek under Sulley's dish lids. "Whatever it is, it smells . . . fishy!"

Sulley batted Mike's hand away. "No peeking. You'll see soon enough."

"Look!" Celia interrupted. "The judges are coming."

A hush fell over the crowd as the judges approached. Each was a famous cooking expert. One was a sushi chef. Another was a famous baker. And the third was the host of a popular barbecue television show.

"Welcome to the Monstropolis Cook-Off!" announced the sushi judge. "As you know, the winner will have their recipe printed in the next issue of *Stomach Churner* magazine. And this year, the top three cooks will also appear on the cover!"

The crowd whispered excitedly as the judges began going from table to table. Celia's snakes dipped the toasted marshmallows in sludge. Celia handed each judge a perfectly sandwiched s'more.

Next, the judges arrived at Mike's table. His cake looked amazing. It was covered with green slime frosting. And Sulley could smell the stinky cabbage all the way from his table. The judges each ate a slice.

"Delicious," one of them said.

"Just the right amount of slime," said another.

Sulley's stomach did a flip. He was up next. Would his entry measure up to Mike's cake and Celia's s'mores?

The judges arrived at Sulley's table. He was pretty nervous! But he believed in his grandmonster's recipes.

With a deep breath, he pulled the lids off his dishes. All three judges gasped. Instead of one recipe, Sulley had made a full meal!

He began serving the judges samples of his food. The first course was cream-of-old-broccoli soup.

"Very stinky," the sushi chef noted.

Next was Grandma Sulley's favorite recipe: slither and onions. It had taken Sulley a while to find the right kind of slugs, but it was worth the effort. The judges smacked their lips.

"Now those are some tasty slugs!" exclaimed the barbecue chef.

For dessert, Sulley handed each judge a fish-tail cupcake.

"Revolting," the pastry chef said. "I'm very impressed."

"Wow, Sulley, you really went all out!" Celia said.

"Yeah, I knew you were cooking up a plan." Mike smiled and nudged his friend.

A short while later, the judges announced the winners. "In third place, we have Mike Wazowski, and his cabbage cake!"

Everyone cheered.

"Great job, Googly Bear!" Celia clapped. Mike winked at Sulley. "See you up there, buddy!" he whispered. Then he trotted up to the podium.

"In second place," the judges said, "is George Sanderson and his slimeburgers."

George looked stunned. "They picked me?" he cried. *"Eeeee!"*

"And in first place," the judges announced, "the winner . . . is James P. Sullivan!"

Sulley's jaw dropped. He had won!

"Way to go!" Mike called as Sulley joined them.

"Yeah, your entry was incredible," added George.

"I couldn't have done it without my grandmonster's cookbook," Sulley said, smiling.

"Here's to Grandma Sulley!" Mike cheered.

That night, Sulley told his grandmonster the good news.

She was thrilled. "I knew you could do it, Sulley-Pie!" she exclaimed.

Sulley was glad he'd made his grandmonster proud.

A few days later, Mike ran into the apartment with the newest issue of *Stomach Churner*.

Sulley, Mike, and George were on the cover, although Mike's face was partly covered by his cabbage cake.

Sulley smiled. "I owe it all to my grandmonster."

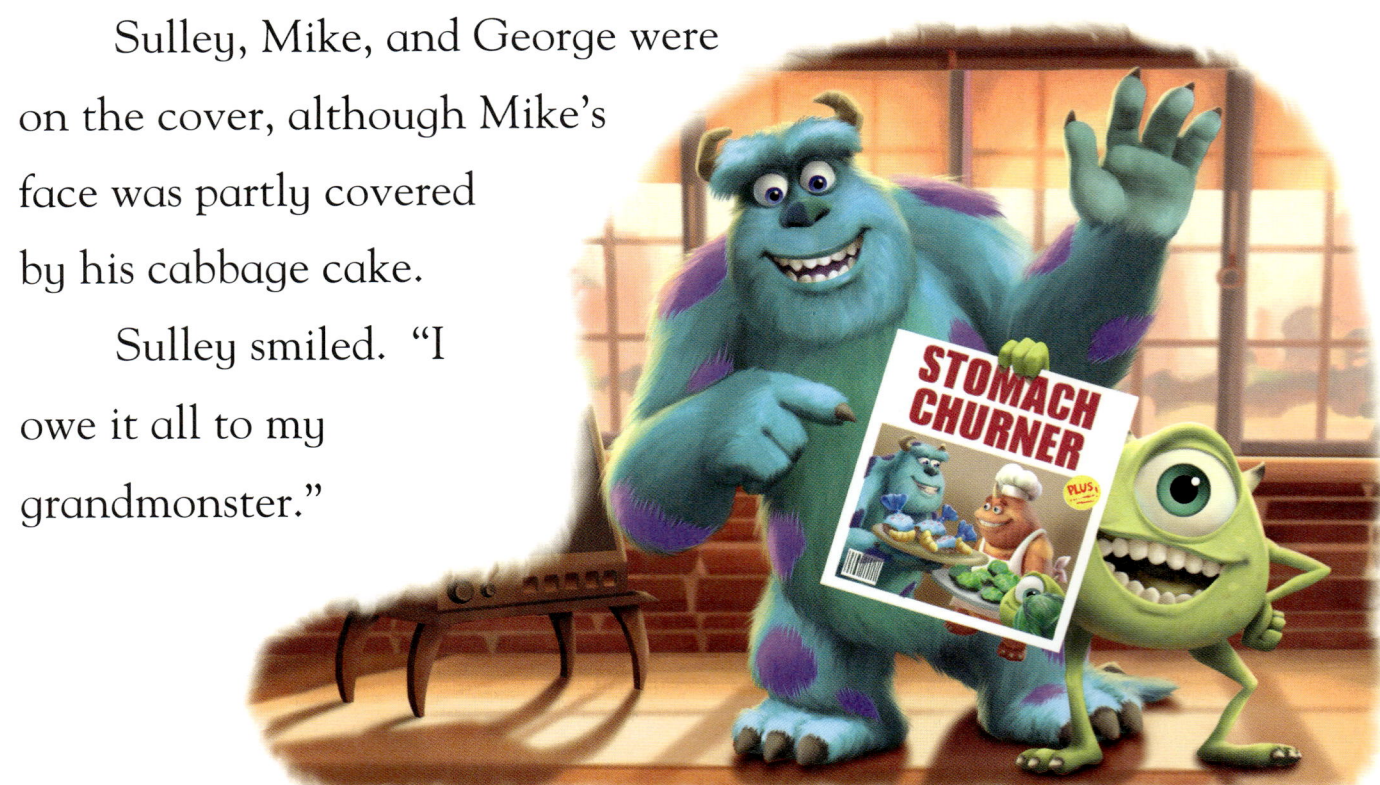

Disney·PIXAR

MONSTERS, INC.

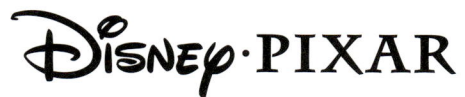

Monster Swim at the Monster Gym

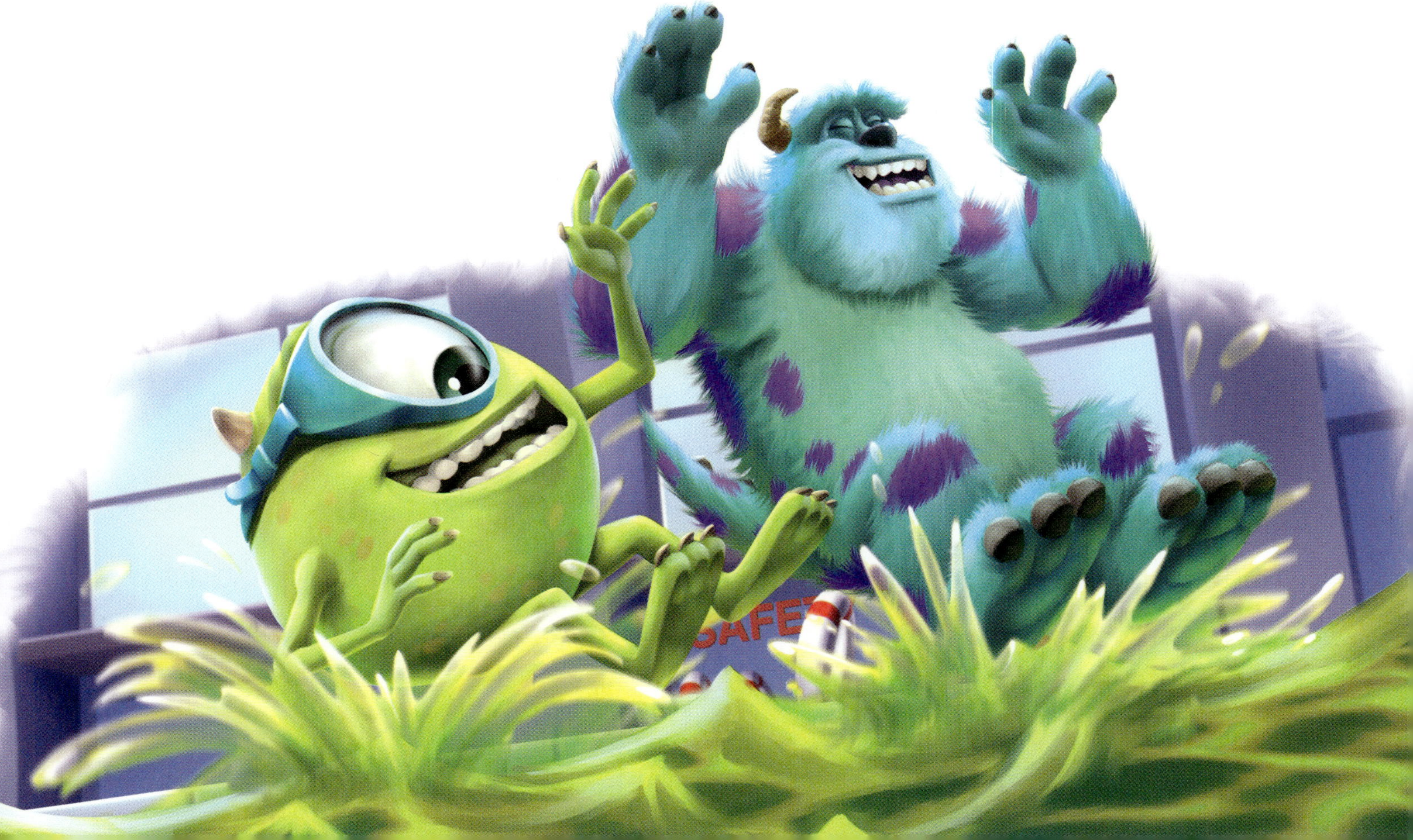

Sulley looked at the clock as he stretched toward the ceiling. Mike was running late. It was the opening weekend at the Monsters, Inc. gym, Supershape.

Everything in the gym was brand-new and sparkling clean. Most of the Laugh Collectors had come to try it out. Some ran on treadmills or rode exercise bikes while others lifted weights. Sulley couldn't wait to get started. Now if only Mike would get here!

The gym was having a contest. Anyone who tried all the different machines and fitness areas during the opening week would be entered to win secret prizes. Four winners would be picked at the end of the week. Sulley had a feeling the prizes would be really nice.

Finally Mike arrived. He was wearing a Supershape sweatband. "What?" Mike asked when Sulley gave him a look. "They were giving away free stuff." Mike shrugged and took a sip from his Supershape water bottle. "Where should we start?"

The friends walked across the gym. Just then, Mike spotted a big, beautiful swimming pool off to one side. Lots of monsters were splashing in the water. "Want to go for a swim?" Mike asked Sulley.

"Look!" Sulley interrupted, pointing out the window. "The track is clear. How about we go there first?"

Mike shrugged and followed Sulley to the outdoor track. They ran several laps, staying in the proper lane.

As they were jogging, Celia hurried over. "Googly Bear, Sulley!" she called. "Come join in my aerobics class!"

Soon everyone was moving to the class's music. "Step, leap! Step, kick!" Celia called out.

Sulley enjoyed bouncing to the rhythm. But Mike was having a hard time keeping up.

"Leap . . . kick . . . step . . . oh, whatever," he finally said. "I'm making up my own moves!"

When aerobics was over, Mike flopped on the floor. "What a workout," he said. "How about a quick dip in the pool to cool off?"

"Or . . . maybe some yoga would make us cool and calm," Sulley suggested.

Mike started to reply, but Sulley pulled him along to the yoga studio. Sulley did the Laughing Lunge, while Mike practiced the Stinky Lotus pose.

Mike didn't mention the pool again until the two friends were sitting at the juice bar. "So what's with you and swimming?" Mike finally asked Sulley. "It's the only thing you don't want to do."

"I don't really like the water," Sulley said, looking down at his smoothie. "It gets my fur all tangled."

"But you want to try to win the contest, right?" Mike asked. "So you have to work out in every part of the gym—and that includes the pool. Just a few laps."

Sulley sighed and followed Mike to the pool. Mike put on his goggle and dove into the deepest part of the water. But Sulley stayed on the stairs at the shallow end. He got his ankles wet first, then his knees.

"It's easier if you go in all at once!" Mike called.

Sulley dipped his paw in the water and splashed a little on his face. The water clung to his fur.

Mike swam up and put his goggle on. "Sulley, can I ask you something? Do you know how to swim?"

Sulley spluttered. "Of course I know how to swim." He paused. "A little bit, anyway." He looked down nervously at the water.

"Everyone needs to know how to swim, pal," Mike said. "I can teach you."

"Oh, you don't have to do that," Sulley said, embarrassed.

"It will be fun!" Mike encouraged him. "We need to come to Supershape anyway if we want to win the prize. How about we end every day with a swimming lesson?"

Sulley sighed. He knew Mike was right. He carefully inched into the pool.

To start, Mike showed him how to blow bubbles through his nose. The first few times that Sulley tried, he came up coughing! But pretty soon Sulley got the hang of it.

The next day, after they had tried a few different areas of the gym, the friends headed to the pool. "Today you're going to lie down on the water," Mike announced.

"You mean float?" Sulley shook his head. "I don't think so."

"Don't worry, pal," Mike said. "The water makes you lighter, so even a big guy like you can do it." He winked. "Just watch."

Sulley took a deep breath and leaned back on Mike's hands. His friend was right. He was floating!

137

Once Sulley was able to float, he could use a kickboard. For the next couple of days, he practiced getting across the pool with it. First he'd hold the board with his front paws and kick with his feet. Then he'd switch it around—he'd put the board under his feet and paddle with his arms.

"You're doing great, pal!" Mike coached him. "You're the fastest furball in the pool!"

"Thanks, Mike," Sulley said. "This is actually kind of fun!" The friends visited the gym twice a day all week, before and after work.

Sometimes they shared the pool with little daycare monsters who were taking swimming classes. But Sulley didn't mind. He liked seeing them laugh and splash. They were having a good time in the water. Sulley was starting to like the water, too.

At the end of the week, Mike made an announcement. "Okay, Sulley," he said. "I think you're ready. It's time to take the plunge!"

"You mean swim by myself?" Sulley asked. "I don't know. . . ."

"You'll be fine!" Mike said. "Just hold on while I get my goggle." He ran to the locker room.

Sulley shivered nervously. Just then, he heard a voice call from across the pool. "Help!"

A little monster was splashing in the water. It looked like he was in trouble! Without even thinking, Sulley jumped in and swam toward him. He sped through the water as fast as he could. He reached the little monster even before the lifeguard did.

Mike returned just in time to see everything. "That was incredible, pal!" he exclaimed. "You swam all by yourself and saved that kid. You were great!"

Sulley smiled. "Yeah, I guess I did."

"Thanks, Mr. Sullivan," the little monster said.

"Anytime," Sulley replied. "But the real hero is Mike. He taught me everything I know."

Later that day, the gym announced the winners of the prizes.

"Thanks to everyone for participating," the head of the gym said. "The winners are: Bile, George, Grunt, and . . . Sulley!"

"Congratulations, pal," Mike said when Sulley came back with his prize envelope. "You earned it. What did you get?"

A wide grin spread over Sulley's face when he opened the envelope. "It's two tickets to the Monstropolis Water Park!" he said. "And I know just who I'm going to take."

Disney · PIXAR

Monsters, Inc.

Mike's Perfect Plan

At exactly six a.m., Mike Wazowski's alarm-clock radio switched on.

"Goooooood morning!" announced the radio deejay.

Mike grunted and pulled his pillow over his ears.

"It's going to be sunny in Monstropolis today," the deejay continued, "just perfect for Valentine's Day."

Mike sat straight up. "That's right. It's Valentine's Day! I've got to get going!"

He swung his legs over the side of the bed and stretched. Then he headed toward the bathroom to take a shower and brush his teeth.

"This is going to be the best day ever!" he told himself in the mirror. Actually, it sounded like, "Thish ish gu ta be she besht thay erer," because his mouth was full of slime toothpaste.

After he showered and sprayed on some cologne, Mike went to the kitchen. He had just enough time for breakfast.

Mike had a big day in store for his girlfriend, Celia. The birthday dinner date he had taken her on a few months earlier had been a disaster. So he wanted to make sure that Valentine's Day would be absolutely perfect. He had been planning for weeks, and hadn't told Celia anything because he wanted her to be surprised.

After a yummy bowl of Prickly Puffs cereal and sour milk, it was time to get started.

Soon, Mike was outside Celia's door. "Happy Valentine's Day, Schmoopsie-Poo," he said, handing her a fresh bouquet of Venus flytrap flowers. "You look lovely as always."

Celia batted her eyelashes and smiled. "Oh, Googly Bear, you shouldn't have," she said. The five snakes that made up her hair—Amelia, Ophelia, Octelia, Bobelia, and Madge—blushed.

"Are you ready to go?" said Mike.

"Where are we going?" Celia asked.

"It's a surprise," Mike replied. "Get ready for the most wonderful day of your life!"

"How exciting!" Celia clapped her hands. "I can't wait."

Mike walked Celia to his car and held the door open for her. Then he hopped in and turned the key. The car made a whirring noise. It wouldn't start.

Mike gave a nervous laugh. "Just a minor delay. Nothing to worry about." He turned the key again and again. But the engine just sputtered.

"I think it might be broken," Celia said.

Mike sighed. If they didn't get going, they would be late for his next surprise. "Come on," he said to Celia, hopping out of the car. "I have an idea."

A few minutes later, they were both aboard the town bus. Unfortunately, it was rush hour. So that meant the bus was crowded. Mike and Celia couldn't get seats together.

"Uh, sorry about this," Mike called across the aisle to Celia. "It wasn't part of the plan."

"It's okay," Celia called back. "At least we're together, sort of."

After a few stops, Mike was finally able to sit by Celia. Suddenly, the bus driver called out, "End of the line!"

Mike looked out the window. "This isn't the right place," he said. "We need to get to Horned Toad Field."

"This is the last stop I make, buddy," said the driver. He pointed to a store up the road. "But I think you can rent bicycles up there, if you want."

"How romantic!" Celia cried. "A bike ride for two!"

"Uh . . . yeah!" Mike said quickly. "That was all part of the grand plan."

Celia and Mike walked up to the store. They noticed a bright pink bike leaning against the wall. It had chipped paint and bent wheels, and was held together with duct tape.

"Let's not get that one," Mike joked.

Two minutes later, they were back outside looking at the sad bike again. It was the only one left to rent. It would have to do.

Mike groaned as he sat in the basket. This was a disaster!

"At least we're closer to each other than we were on the bus," Celia offered cheerfully.

Finally, Mike and Celia reached their destination.

"Surprise!" Mike exclaimed.

Celia looked up to see a large hot-air balloon. "Oh, Michael," she gasped. "I've never been in a hot-air balloon before!"

Mike puffed out his chest proudly. "That's me—Mr. Romantic!"

They climbed into the basket, and Mike turned on the fan to blow hot air into the balloon. Soon, they were soaring high above Monstropolis.

Mike smiled. "Happy Valentine's Day, Celia," he said. But then he noticed something was very, very wrong. Celia's snakes were shaking, and their eyes had grown huge. "What's wrong with them?" he asked, pointing at the snakes.

"I've never seen them act like this," Celia said. "I think they're afraid of heights!"

The snakes started panicking. They began to hiss and flail around. The balloon began to rock and sway!

"I'm taking us down!" Mike yelled. He quickly let out some air from the balloon. But he wasn't moving fast enough for the scared snakes. Two of them reached up and took big bites out of the balloon's side.

WHOOSH!

Mike, Celia, and the balloon crashed through a grove of leafy trees and into some prickly bushes. The snakes sighed with relief. But Celia and Mike were covered in spiky thistles!

Mike felt terrible as he and Celia walked back to the bus stop. "I'm sorry," he said. "I had no idea your snakes were afraid of heights. Today isn't really 'taking off' the way I had hoped."

Celia giggled at Mike's joke. "It's okay," she said. "It was still a nice idea."

"This was supposed to be the best Valentine's Day ever," Mike said, frustrated. "I had the perfect plan."

"Oh, Mike, you don't have to—" Celia began.

"But I'm not out of ideas yet!" Mike added quickly. "Just you wait— there's still one BIG surprise left. You'll see. It will be amazing!"

That evening, Mike picked up Celia and told her his last surprise. "I have two tickets for the Monster Ballet."

"Ooh!" cooed Celia. "Those tickets are impossible to get!"

"Nothing is impossible for Googly Bear," he said.

At the theater, Mike and Celia went to their seats.

"I think I might be a little overdressed," Celia whispered.

Mike looked around at the audience. Celia was right. Some of the monsters were dressed a bit . . . unusually.

Mike looked down at his ticket. His eye grew wide. It said Monster *Battle*, not Monster *Ballet*!

Just then, a spotlight shone on an announcer in the center of a wrestling ring. "Get ready to . . . GRUMBLE!" he shouted.

The crowd roared. Two monsters came to the center of the ring. A giant screen flashed their names: André the Furry and Dragonbreath McSnarl.

"Mon-ster Bat-tle! Mon-ster Bat-tle!" chanted the crowd.

The bell rang, and the match was on!

André moved quickly and bounced off the ropes. Then he leaped into the air and slammed into Dragonbreath. The monster went flying across the ring.

"OOF!" exclaimed the crowd.

But Dragonbreath McSnarl quickly lifted André up over his head, and spun him around with a roar.

"McSnarl! McSnarl!" the audience yelled.

Mike buried his head in his hands. "I'm so sorry, Celia," he said. "Nothing today turned out the way it was supposed to. I ruined Valentine's Day." But as he got up to leave, he was shocked to see Celia cheering along with the crowd!

"Celia, I didn't know you liked wrestling," Mike exclaimed. "It's not romantic at all."

Celia shrugged and smiled. "As long as we're together, I don't mind what we do. Besides, this is kind of exciting!"

Mike couldn't believe it! After all the mistakes they'd had that day, Celia was happy just to be with him. Grinning, he called out to a vendor. "Two monster ices over here, please!"

Drinks in hand, Mike and Celia settled back to cheer on the wrestlers along with the rest of the crowd.

Now that I know she likes wrestling, I can't wait until her birthday, Mike said to himself as his sipped his drink. It's going to be the most perfect plan ever!

DISNEY·PIXAR
MONSTERS, INC.
A Monstrous Mess of a Party

Sulley was always happy when he visited Boo in the human world. But one night, he had a lot on his mind.

"I have a problem," he told Boo. "I've been so busy at work, I haven't planned anything for Mike's birthday. And it's in two days!"

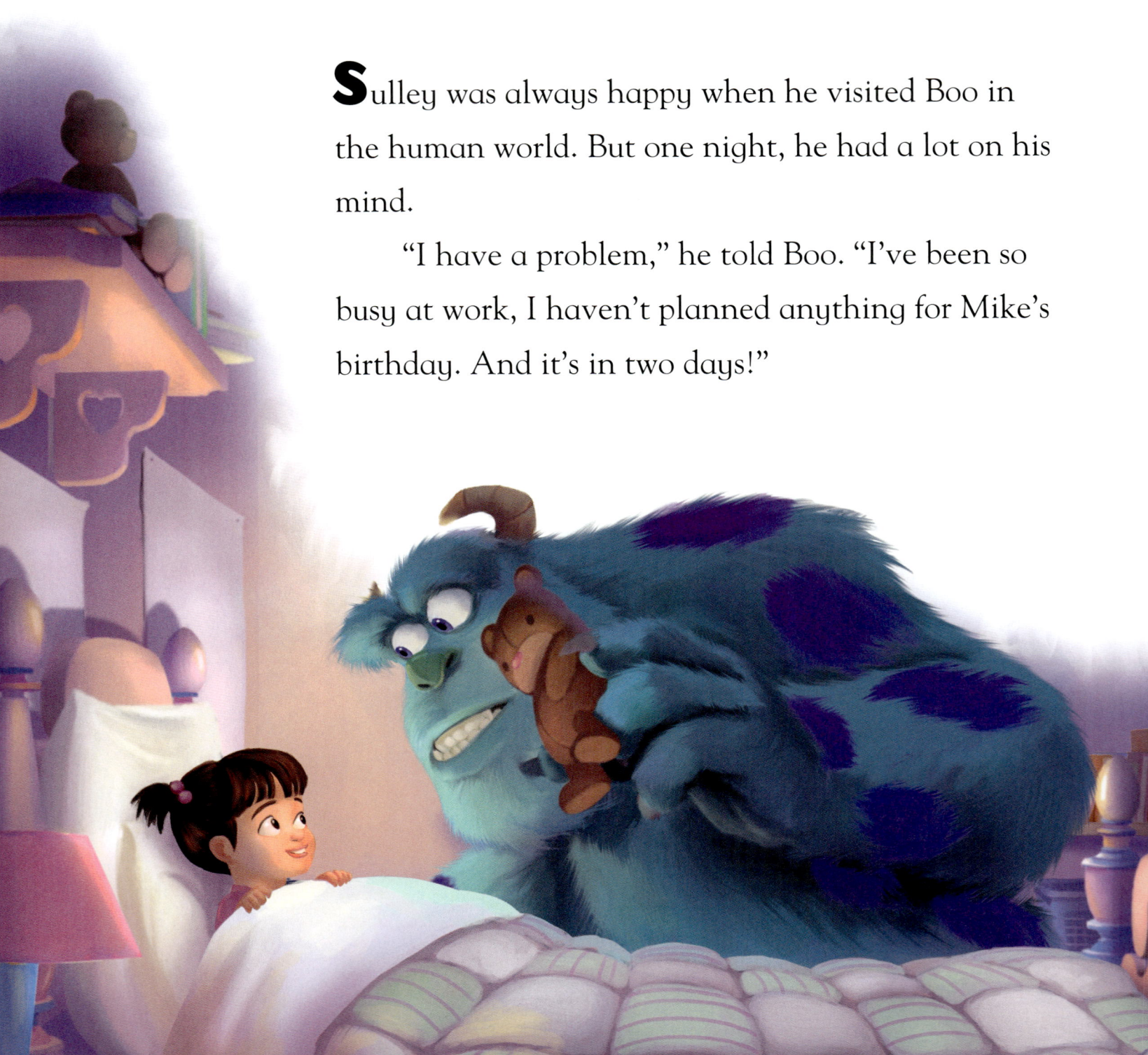

"I always plan something special," Sulley continued. "Last year I took Mike to see a giant chunk of stinky cheese. He loved it!" Sulley sighed. "I don't know what I'm going to do."

Boo's eyes lit up. "Party!" she cried.

She hurried to her dresser and handed Sulley a picture.

"Party, huh?" Sulley said. He looked at the picture, which had been taken at Boo's last birthday party. Boo was next to a big cake, and kids were playing all kinds of games. Sulley had been to monster birthdays with slime sundaes and scary movie marathons. But he had never seen a party like the one in Boo's photo.

"I think Mike would love this!" Sulley exclaimed. "May I borrow this picture?"

The next morning, Sulley showed his friends the photo. Mike's girlfriend, Celia, was there, along with George Sanderson, Smitty, Needleman, and Chalooby, who oozed slime wherever he went.

"I want to throw a party like this for Mike's birthday," Sulley explained.

"It looks fun," Celia said. "But how do we make it?"

"We can gather the supplies today," Sulley said, "and surprise Mike tomorrow when he gets home from work. What do you say?"

That afternoon, each of the friends set out with a copy of Boo's picture and a job to do. Smitty and Needleman had volunteered to make the cake.

"What are those things?" Smitty asked, pointing to the birthday candles in the picture.

Needleman shrugged. "I don't know. Maybe they're worms?"

The friends agreed that that must be what they were. So they headed off to the Monstropolis Swamp.

Needleman grabbed a handful of worms from the mud and dropped them into his pail. "Now for some sludge!" he said excitedly.

"You're having all the fun!" Smitty complained. He tried to get in front of Needleman to grab some worms, too. But when he moved, he slipped on the mud.

SPLAT! They both fell face-first into the muck! "Oh, great," Needleman said. "My mud bath is usually on Tuesday."

Back at Monsters, Inc., George looked at his copy of Boo's photo. His job was to make something similar to the piñata. But he had never seen one before, so he didn't know what it was.

Maybe it's a stuffed monster, he thought, heading to the daycare closets. Soon, he'd picked out a toy monster.

"You're awfully cute," he said, stuffing it into his bag.

Celia was in charge of presents. She was supposed to pick out a different gift for each of Mike's friends to give him.

But she couldn't pull herself away from the aftershave counter at Monster Mart. Everything smelled so wonderful! Boiled Cabbage had a nice stink to it. So did Rotten Milk. And Dog Breath! Her snakes just loved the way Dog Breath aftershave smelled.

"I'll take ten boxes of Dog Breath," she told the salesmonster.

Down the street, Sulley was picking out games at the Monstropolis toy store. He put Pin the Forked Tail on the Monster in his shopping cart, along with Monster Bowling.

Then he checked Boo's picture. The kids in the photo were tossing around a large red disk. He asked the store owner for help finding something like it.

"Why are they throwing a plate?" she asked, confused. Sulley shrugged and decided to try the kitchen store.

The next afternoon, the friends set up for the party. George used a string to hang his stuffed monster from the ceiling.

"How does that look, Sulley?" he asked.

"Great," Sulley said. "Now just grab the bat."

"Bat?" George blinked. He looked at Boo's picture and gasped. A boy was whacking the animal with a bat! He didn't realize that a piñata was a paper animal filled with candy.

"Uh . . . right . . . bat . . ." he said. "You got it!" He then hid the bat. He didn't want anyone hitting his stuffed monster! Suddenly, the kitchen door flew open.

Chalooby slid through the door, leaving behind a trail of slime. He was carrying a bowl of punch that was sloshing everywhere.

"Here comes the cake!" Needleman cried.

He and Smitty carried in a towering plate of chocolatey goop with worms sticking out.

"You were supposed to make it look like this," Sulley said, pointing to the cake in Boo's picture.

"We tried!" Smitty said. "But the worms wouldn't go into the oven, so we couldn't bake it."

Sulley compared Boo's picture to the messy room. What he and his friends had put together looked more like a disaster than a party!

Suddenly, the friends heard a key in the lock.

"Oh, no!" Sulley exclaimed. "That's got to be Mike! I hope he likes it."

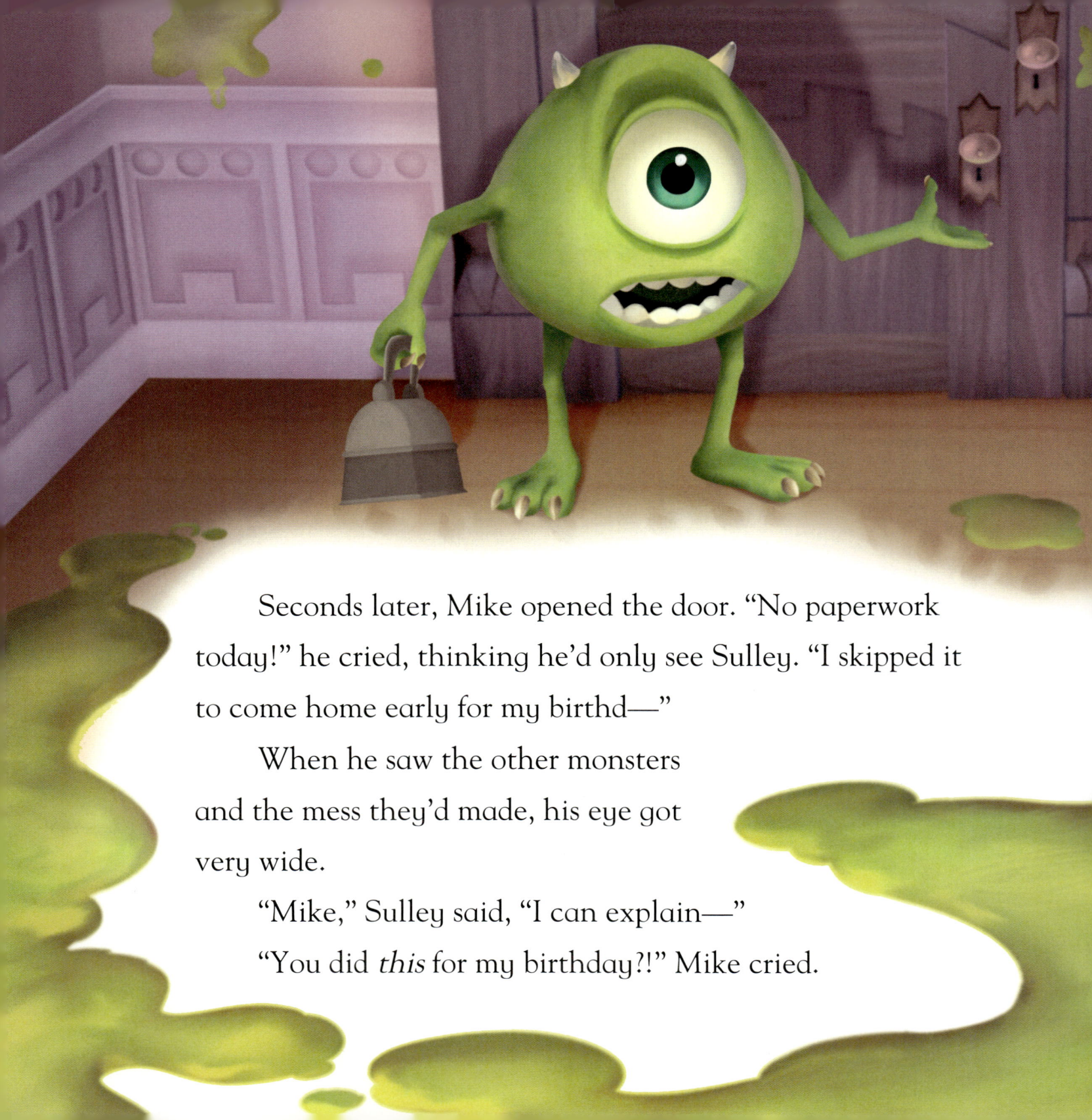

Seconds later, Mike opened the door. "No paperwork today!" he cried, thinking he'd only see Sulley. "I skipped it to come home early for my birthd—"

When he saw the other monsters and the mess they'd made, his eye got very wide.

"Mike," Sulley said, "I can explain—"

"You did *this* for my birthday?!" Mike cried.

"It's *amazing*!" Mike pointed to the slime and punch spilled on the floor. "Oh, boy! A slime-slide!" He dove into it. Green goo splashed everywhere!

The other monsters looked at each other, wondering if they should explain. But Mike looked like he was having so much fun.

Finally, Sulley shrugged and said, "Come on, everybody! Let's play on the slime-slide!" Then he ran and slid along it himself.

Soon all the monsters were sliding and laughing together!

Eventually, Mike noticed the stack of plates and hurried over.

"Cool—a plate toss!" he exclaimed. He threw the top plate against the wall, and it smashed. Soon, the friends were competing to see who could break the most plates. Mike won!

"Is this my prize for winning?" Mike asked, pointing at the stuffed monster hanging from the ceiling. He jumped up and down to try to reach it.

"Don't hurt him!" George cried, anxiously. He was glad Mike hadn't said anything about a bat.

Meanwhile, Needleman was feeling hot. So he dunked his head in the punch bowl. "Ooh!" he said. "Refreshing!"

Later, Mike opened his presents. Everyone agreed the Dog Breath aftershave smelled very nice on him.

They even tried the cake, which turned out to be quite tasty after all!

"This is the best birthday ever, guys!" Mike exclaimed.

The next night, Sulley visited Boo again. "Thanks for lending me this," he said, handing her picture back. "It was a huge help."

"Party for Mike Wazowski?" Boo asked.

"That's right," Sulley said. He showed Boo a photo they'd taken at Mike's party.

Sulley smiled. "It may not have turned out exactly right," he said. "But Mike thought it was perfect."

Disney · PIXAR

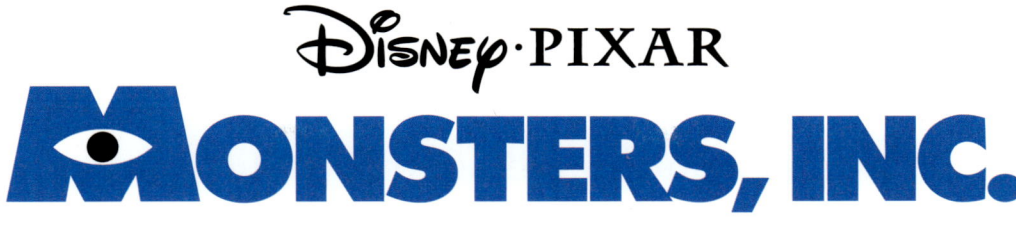

MONSTERS, INC.

An Abominable Vacation

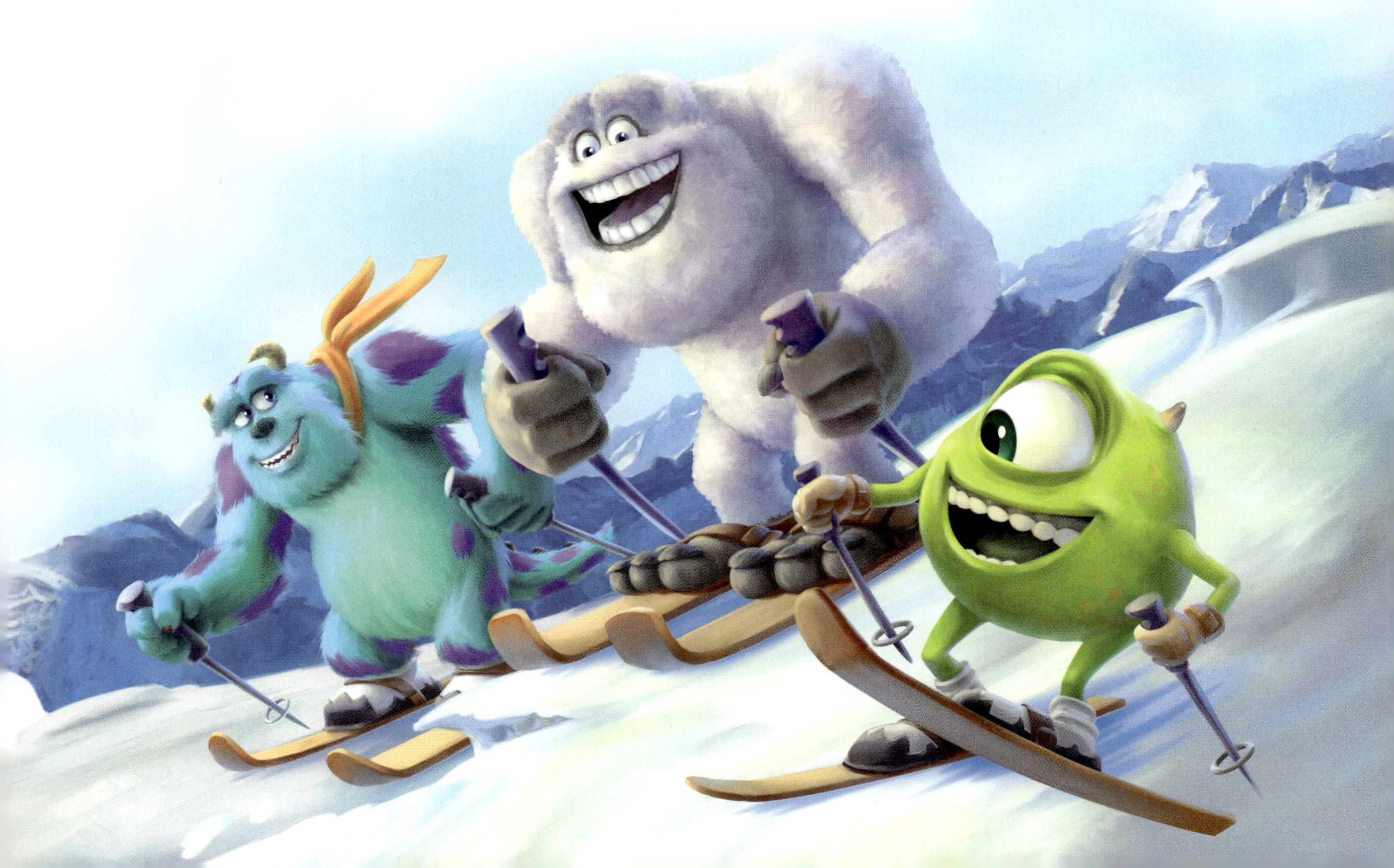

Mike, Sulley, and Celia chatted happily as they strolled down the sidewalk. It was a beautiful day. The sun was shining. There wasn't a cloud in the sky. And best of all, the three friends had a whole week off from work!

Every year, during the warmer months, Monsters, Inc. would close for a few days so their employees could have a chance to relax. Some monsters went on trips. Others stayed in town and had Monstropoly board-game marathons. The local movie theater made sure there were lots of scary movies playing.

But this year was special. Sulley, Mike, and Celia were going to take a vacation together.

The problem was, they still hadn't decided where to go.

"We could head to Swampy Beach," Mike suggested. "Kick back and soak up some sun."

"I'd rather do something more exciting," Celia said as the three friends crossed the street.

"We could go skydiving!" Mike offered.

"That sounds *too* exciting," Sulley said.

They trooped up the stairs to the guys' apartment. Just then, Celia eyed a magazine on Mike and Sulley's sofa. It was called *Extreme Monster Sports.* "What about a ski trip?" she asked.

"That's perfect!" Mike said excitedly, picking up the magazine. "And you know who we could visit?" He turned to Sulley.

"The Abominable Snowman!" they said at the same time.

The Abominable Snowman was a large monster with thick white fur. He lived all alone in the Himalaya mountains—in the human world. Mike and Sulley had met him once before, and the three had become friends. They were glad they had a chance to visit him!

Mike ran to the closet to start packing. "Skis, boots, gloves, goggles, first-aid kit," he called, tossing everything to Sulley. "This is going to be the best vacation ever!"

The next morning, Sulley, Mike, and Celia used a closet door from Monsters, Inc. to travel to the Himalayas.

"Do you think he'll mind that we've come to visit?" Sulley asked when they reached the Abominable Snowman's cave.

Just then, their friend came to the entrance. "Mike? Sulley?" he said in surprise. Then, he scooped all three of them up in a bear hug. "My old friends!"

"He doesn't mind!" Mike grinned.

There was a lot for the friends to catch up on. Mike and Sulley told Abominable all about their adventure with Boo. And Celia loved hearing about life in the human world.

But most of all, Abominable couldn't wait to show his friends around the Himalayas. They hiked to the top of a tall mountain and skied all the way down. They made hot yak's-milk cocoa. They even built snowmonsters!

On the last night of their visit, the four friends sat around a fire and told spooky stories.

"And that was the last time those brave monsters ever saw that awful child," the Abominable Snowman said, finishing his tale. "But they say, late at night, you can still hear the eerie sound of its laughter. The sound . . . of evil."

Mike, Sulley, and Celia looked at one another.

"You know, Abominable," Sulley started, "it turns out children aren't as bad as we thought. They're not dangerous."

"Yeah," Mike said. "A lot has changed in Monstropolis since you were last there. Monsters, Inc. collects laughs now."

"Really?" Abominable asked. He looked sad for a moment. "I wish I could come back to visit."

"But you can!" Mike cried. "Sulley's in charge of Monsters, Inc. now. You can visit whenever you want."

"Come back with us tomorrow!" Celia exclaimed.

The next morning, the four friends went back to Monstropolis. The streets were packed with monsters strolling and shopping.

"Wow," said Abominable, "I'd forgotten how busy it is here." He glanced up at the sun. "And warm. My fur's getting itchy."

"Don't worry, pal," Mike said. "The next stop on your tour of Monstropolis just happens to be the perfect place to cool down."

Soon the gang was seated in the Cinescare movie theater. A new film, *Goon with the Wind*, was playing.

"You're going to love this," Mike whispered to Abominable. "Scarlett O'Hairy is a great actress."

Abominable nodded. He felt much cooler. But he had trouble eating his popcorn. It kept sticking to his woolly fur. "I guess I'm used to all my food being frozen," he said.

When the movie was finished, the friends went to get dinner. Mike, Celia, and Sulley wanted to impress Abominable, so they took him to a fancy restaurant.

They helped him order from the long menu. First was a rotten-vegetable appetizer, followed by stewed slugs and stinky-cheese soup.

When it was time to order dessert, Abominable knew just what he wanted. "I'd like a snow cone, please," he said.

"I'm afraid we don't serve those," the waiter replied. "But may I recommend the moldy banana cake surprise? It's *very* impressive."

When the dessert came out, Abominable was stunned. The banana cake certainly was a surprise! It was enormous, with slime frosting dripping down the sides and sparklers on top.

"Bet you can't get that in the Himalayas!" Mike exclaimed. But Abominable didn't look very excited.

The next morning, Mike, Celia, and Sulley took Abominable to the Monstropolis Art Museum. The friends admired some famous paintings by well-known monster artists. But Mike and Sulley could tell Abominable was feeling down.

"Do you think he doesn't like museums?" Mike whispered.

Sulley shrugged. "Maybe we should ask him what's wrong."

Back at Mike and Sulley's apartment, Abominable explained that he was feeling homesick. "I've been having a great time," he said. "But I think it's time for me to go back to the Himalayas."

"You know you don't have to live alone in the human world anymore," Mike said. "You could stay in Monstropolis."

Abominable smiled. "I know. But I miss my cave and the snow. I even miss the icicles that form inside my nose."

"Well, when you put it like that, who could argue?" Mike said.

The next morning, the friends all went to the Laugh Floor at Monsters, Inc. to wish Abominable good-bye.

"We'll come visit again next year," Sulley said.

"I can't wait!" Abominable answered.

Later, as the Abominable Snowman relaxed at his cave, he took a deep breath of cold mountain air. His nose immediately filled with icicles.

"Ahhh," he said. "It's good to be home."

MONSTERS, INC.
Monster Laughs

James P. Sullivan looked at the monthly energy charts. As the head of Monsters, Inc., it was his job to make sure the power levels stayed high. That meant the other monsters had to collect a lot of laughter so it could be converted into energy. But lately none of the monsters seemed to be getting enough laughs. Sulley was worried.

He went to the Laugh Floor and peeked through a closet door. It opened to a little boy's room, where Pauley was telling a joke.

"Aw, I've heard that one before," the boy said with a yawn.

Sulley closed the door quietly. Pauley was usually one of the top Laugh Collectors.

Lanky walked through another door. "A kid threw a glass
of milk at me and then fell asleep! It was awful!" he said.

At lunchtime, Sulley and his best friend Mike shared a gooey pizza with extra tentacles.

"Mikey, we've got a problem," Sulley said. "The monsters just aren't funny anymore. All their routines are old and dull. And that means we aren't collecting enough laughs."

Mike thought for a moment. "I got it!" he said, snapping his fingers. "I'll write some new jokes and gags."

Mike spent the next few nights working on all kinds of new material.

Mike performed for the other monsters. He told jokes about his eye. He showed them a juggling act with chattering teeth . . .

Mike burped out a beautiful ballad . . . and he pretended to be a bowling ball.

When he finished his act, Mike handed out scripts to each of the monsters. "Just perform the jokes the way I did and you'll have those kids laughing so hard they'll be falling out of their beds!"

That night, Pauley tried one of Mike's jokes. "Why did the one-eyed monster have to close his school?" he asked. "Because he only had one pupil!"

But the girl couldn't take her eyes off all of Pauley's eyes.

Ricky was having problems of his own. The chattering teeth were too small for his mouth!

And Spike tried the bowling ball routine, but he stuck to the floor.

"What an awful night!" Lanky exclaimed as he left the Laugh Floor.

But then . . . WHOOPS! He slipped on a banana peel and flew into the air. When he landed, he looked like a pretzel! Lanky and all the other monsters howled with laughter.

"That's it!" Mike exclaimed. "Instead of copying me, you just have to be yourselves. Then the kids will laugh."

Mike helped each monster come up with his own jokes.

He told Pauley to pop out some of his eyes.

"Oops, sorry . . . don't mean to roll my eyes at you," said Pauley.

"Perfect!" Mike exclaimed.

Next, Mike helped Spike come up with some new tricks.

A few days later, the Laugh Floor buzzed with activity. The new jokes were working!

"Great job, Mikey. Power levels are back up!" said Sulley.

Mike beamed. He couldn't have been prouder of the other monsters.

"I didn't do anything," he said. "These guys are naturals."

As Mike headed toward a door, Sulley stopped him. "Hey, Mike, what do you call a green monster with one eye and a big mouth?"

"Unbelievably good looking?" Mike asked.

"Hilarious!" said Sulley.

"Thanks, pal," said Mike. He twirled his microphone, and strode through the door. "Showtime!"

MONSTERS, INC.

Making the Team

Mike and Sulley were having a picnic in Monstropolis Park. It was a beautiful spring day. "I love this time of year," Mike said. "The birds are singing, the flowers are blooming . . ."

". . . and monsterball season is on its way," Sulley finished for him. The friends glanced over at a group of monsters playing monsterball nearby.

"Boy, do I love that game." Mike smiled. In monsterball, two teams both tried to keep a ball in the air on one side of a net. But the court was covered in mud, and there was a slime pit on each side. Players sometimes had to jump over it to hit the ball.

"Tryouts for the Monsters, Inc. team are starting soon," Sulley said. "Should we sign up?"

"I don't know," Mike said. "I was pretty embarrassed after last year's tryouts. Remember how I kept missing the monsterball?"

"Then I knocked George Sanderson into the slime pit," Sulley said.

"And I went flying in the wrong direction!" Mike said, laughing. "The other team thought I was helping them win!"

"Yeah," Sulley agreed. "You can hardly blame them for not letting us on the team."

Mike nodded. "But we still went to every game."

"It was a good season," Sulley said. "The Monsters, Inc. team almost won the championship!"

"And we were there for it, cheering from the bleachers." Mike frowned. "But, man, I wish we could have been in on the action."

Sulley thought for a moment. "What do you say we go all out this year? We'll train real hard for tryouts and everything."

"I say we start training right now!" Mike said excitedly.

Mike and Sulley spent the rest of the day playing monsterball in the park. They practiced their jumps, their mud slides, and their slime-pit leaps. Soon, they were both tired out.

"I wonder if we're any better now?" Mike said. He was lying flat on his back, panting.

"How could we tell?" Sulley said. He flopped down beside Mike on the soft grass.

"I know just what we need," Mike said. "A coach!"

The next day, Mike started calling around to see if anyone knew a good monsterball coach. He called his sister, his cousin, and his next-door neighbor. But no one was able to help. So, he also tried his girlfriend, Celia, then her cousin, his sister's best friend, and Celia's cousin's sister's best friend.

Finally, Mike struck gold. Celia's cousin's sister's best friend's neighbor knew just the monster for the job!

"The coach will be here first thing tomorrow morning!" Mike said with a big smile.

The next morning, Sulley and Mike took extra time getting themselves ready.

Mike wondered what the coach would be like. Would he have many arms and legs? (Monsters with lots of arms were often good at monsterball.) Would he be tough, like a drill sergeant? Or would he be nice?

Whoever it was, the friends could hardly wait!

The doorbell rang. Sulley ran to the door and flung it open.

And there stood . . . Roz!

"Good morning, boys," she grumbled.

"R-R-R-Roz!" Mike stammered.

"You're the monsterball coach?" Sulley asked.

"That's me," Roz said. She slid in. "And you two are in serious need of coaching."

She pointed at the floor. "Push-ups," she said. "One hundred. Now." Mike and Sulley looked at each other and got on the floor.

After the push-ups, there was an hour of monster-tossing practice. Sulley would throw Mike into the air as high as he could and then catch him. In the afternoon, Roz had Mike work on his slime-pit leaps while Sulley perfected his mud slide.

They finished the day with something Roz called "cross-training." This meant Sulley had to juggle a chair, a bowl of cereal, and Mike—while Mike was knitting a scarf. They ended up in a heap on the ground.

"Was that really necessary?" Mike asked.

"For every question, you'll give me a hundred push-ups," Roz said. "Start counting, Wazowski."

222

The next day was even worse.

More leaping, more tossing, more sliding—and that was just in the morning. In the afternoon, Roz finally let them play an actual game of monsterball. But she yelled at them nonstop.

"You aim like a blind mole, Sullivan," she told Sulley.

"I've seen icebergs move faster, Wazowski," she told Mike.

"I'm starting to think," Mike said, trying to catch his breath, "that this was a big mistake."

But it wasn't very long before Mike was leaping over the slime pit with ease and Sulley could slide fast enough to reach a monsterball all the way on the other side of the court.

"I think we're getting better, Mike," Sulley said.

"All right, boys," Roz called. "Show me what you got." She tossed a monsterball at them, and the game was on.

Mud went flying as Sulley slid to reach the monsterball and whacked it over the net. And Mike was able to bat it away from the slime pit every time. The ball came whizzing back down, and they both jumped high into the air.

"Well," Roz said. She paused to polish her glasses. "I have been *more* disappointed in my life."

"I think," Mike whispered to Sulley, "that means she's *proud*."

On the day of the tryouts, Mike and Sulley were feeling good. "I really think we'll make the team," Sulley said.

But when they walked onto the court, Mike's heart sank. "Is it just me, or does it look like everyone else has been training, too?" he whispered to Sulley.

There was a monster with tentacles juggling six balls. Several monsters were doing push-ups— on one anothers' backs. And one monster leaped over the slime pit and landed on the other side of the net.

The coach blew his whistle. All the monsters trying out for the team gathered around him. He divided them into two groups and tossed the monsterball between them. The tryouts had begun.

Mike and Sulley played hard. They did everything they could to keep the ball from touching the ground. At one point, Sulley even tossed Mike into the air high enough to smack the ball straight down onto the other team's side. The coach was impressed!

"Great tryouts, everyone," the coach said. "After seeing you all play, I've decided who will be on the team this year."

Sulley and Mike looked at each other. This was the moment they had been waiting for! One by one, the coach began calling names. Before long, there were hardly any spots left.

". . . Sanderson," the coach said. He looked at his clipboard.

"And finally," the coach called, "Sullivan and Wazowski!" Mike and Sulley high-fived. They had made the team!

"That was good playing today," the coach said to Mike and Sulley. "I hear you've been practicing with Roz."

"She's the best!" Mike said.

"Now, there's a monster who knows the value of cross-training." The coach smiled. "Okay, team—grab your knitting needles!"

Mike and Sulley groaned as monsters got items to juggle for cross-training.

"Here we go again!" Sulley said.

One month later, Mike was flying through the air. It was the first monsterball game of the season.

"Wheee!" Mike yelled as Sulley threw him toward the incoming monsterball.

Whack! Mike smacked the ball back at the other team. As he sailed through the air, he spotted a familiar face in the crowd. It was Roz!

"Thanks, Roz!" he yelled. "We owe it all to *youuuuuu!*"

MONSTERS, INC.

The Mysterious Prankster

"**I**'m so excited to go to work with you today, Uncle Mike!" Joey said, jumping up and down. The little monster could hardly keep still as he and his uncle stood at the corner waiting for the light to change.

Joey's parents were out of town, and Mike had offered to watch his nephew for the day while they were away.

"Me, too," Mike said with a smile. "I think you're really going to make a lot of friends in daycare."

Joey's face fell. "Awwww. I thought I was going to go on the Laugh Floor with you today. I want to learn everything there is to know about making human kids laugh!"

Mike patted his nephew on the head. "I have to do some work today, kiddo. But I promise we'll have lunch together. And we can play after work."

Joey didn't say anything as he and his uncle crossed the street. But he looked very disappointed.

When Mike dropped Joey off at the daycare room, his nephew began to cry.

"Please take me with you," Joey begged. "I really, really, really want to be a Laugh Collector just like you, Uncle Mike! I'm very funny!"

"I'm sorry, Joey," said Mike. "But I've got to get to work. I'll come pick you up at lunchtime, I promise!"

Mike walked down the hallway to drop off some overdue paperwork at the office. As he waited in line, he started to feel bad about leaving Joey. I'll make it up to him, he thought. Maybe if I fill my laugh quota quickly today, I can pick up Joey early.

That made Mike feel better. He headed to the locker room to prepare for a busy day of laugh collecting.

"Goooood morning, Sulley," Mike said to his big, furry best friend.

"'Morning, Mike," said Sulley. "Did you get Joey off to daycare okay?"

"I did, although he wasn't very happy about it," Mike said as he reached up to open his locker. But though he tugged and tugged, he just couldn't get it open. It was stuck!

"Need some help, buddy?" asked Sulley. "Why don't I . . ."

Just then, the locker opened. To Mike's astonishment, he was hit in the face by an avalanche of table tennis balls, which started bouncing all over the room! *Boing, boing, boing!*

"Yikes!" said Mike.

"That was weird," said Sulley, trying hard not to laugh. "Where did those come from?"

Mike shrugged. "I have no idea. But that was some practical joke. Whoever it was got me good!"

Mike was still shaking his head as he walked onto the Laugh Floor. Who could have played that joke on him?

Suddenly, he noticed a monster's purple tail disappearing around a corner. That tail looks familiar, Mike thought. He went to see who it was, but the monster was gone.

Mike shrugged and started work on the Laugh Floor. Soon, he was collecting laughs fast and furious.

At this rate, I'll be able to pick up Joey in no time, Mike thought. But as he stepped forward, he suddenly began to slide.

"Ay, chihuahua!" he cried.

Thump! He landed right on his bottom.

Mike had slipped on a banana peel! "All right," he said. "I'll admit, that was pretty funny. Who did it?"

But no one would take credit for the practical joke.

"Strange," Mike said, as he went for a drink of water. "If I didn't know any better, I'd think . . . *ahhhhhh*!" The water fountain squirted him!

"These jokes aren't funny anymore," Mike said. "It's like someone is out to get me." He gasped. "You know, I wonder if it has anything to do with that monster's tail!"

Suddenly, he remembered why it had seemed familiar. "It looked like Randall's tail!" Mike exclaimed.

Randall was a former coworker who had been banished for trying to kidnap a human child. Mike and Sulley had stopped him. If Randall had returned, one of the first monsters he would want revenge on would be Mike!

"He's got to be the one playing all these awful jokes on me!" Mike said. "I need to tell Sulley about this."

It was lunchtime, so Mike knew he would see Sulley in the cafeteria. But first, he headed to daycare to pick up Joey.

"Has your day been full of laughs, Uncle Mike?" Joey asked.

"Not exactly," answered Mike.

"Hey Schmoopsie-Poo!" a monster called out to him.

"That was weird," said Mike. Only Celia ever called him Schmoopsie-Poo. Why would another monster say that to him?

When Mike and Joey reached the cafeteria, Sulley waved to them from across the room. "I saved you two seats!" he called.

"Sulley," Mike whispered when they reached the table. "Someone has been playing practical jokes on me all day. And I think it could be Randall! I'm pretty sure I saw his tail disappear around a corner earlier today on the Laugh Floor."

Sulley laughed. "Mike, you have the craziest imagination! Let's go get lunch." They all loaded up their plates with food. But when they sat down, more strange things started to happen.

The sugar Mike put in his coffee was actually salt. When Joey passed Mike the rotten-tomato ketchup, the top fell off. And when Mike tried to pick up his fork, it was glued to the table!

Worst of all, when Mike came back to the table after getting dessert, someone had put a whoopee cushion on his chair. It made a really embarrassing noise.

BRRRRT!

"That sure was funny, wasn't it, Uncle Mike?" Joey laughed.

"That's it!" said Mike, throwing down the whoopee cushion. "Sulley, we've got to talk."

Sulley nodded. "We have to get to the bottom of this," he said.

Mike brought Joey to daycare and went to Sulley's office.

"You really think that Randall has returned?" Sulley asked, frowning. "But why?"

"For revenge!" Mike explained.

Sulley shook his head. "I'm still not sure," he said. "It's not like Randall to play practical jokes."

"He's messing with me," Mike insisted. "He thinks these tricks are driving me crazy. But I know how we can find out if he's back. We have to set a trap!"

So the two friends came up with a plan. Mike would pretend to take a nap in the Laugh Simulator room. No practical joker would be able to resist playing a trick on him! When the prankster was next to the bed, Sulley would release a net to trap the culprit.

Mike rubbed his hands together. "I just know it's Randall!" he said. He stepped out of Sulley's office and yawned loudly. "I'm going to take a quick nap!" he announced. He went to the Laugh Simulator room, climbed into bed, and closed his eye.

Zzzzzz! A few minutes later, Mike really was asleep!

Luckily, Sulley was there, and he was still awake. When the practical joker snuck up to the bed holding some shaving cream, Sulley yanked the rope.

"Gotcha!" cried Sulley.

Mike woke up with a start. He reached over and switched on the bedside light. But the prankster wasn't Randall at all. . . .

It was Mike's nephew—Joey!

"Joey?" said Mike, shocked. "You're the prankster?"

"I wanted to show you that I would make a great Laugh Collector," Joey said, smiling. "So I played jokes on you all day. I hid under this." He held up a purple blanket. It was the "tail" Mike thought he'd seen earlier!

Mike and Sulley couldn't help but laugh.

"Joey has talent," Sulley told Mike. "And best of all . . ."

". . . Randall isn't really back!" the two friends said together.

Disney·PIXAR
MONSTERS, INC.
Who's That Monster?

Mike walked to Sulley's office. It was time for the two best friends to head to the gym for their morning workout. But Sulley's office door was shut.

Mike was surprised. Sulley always kept his door open. He reached up to knock.

"Not so fast, Mr. Wazowski," said Sulley's assistant, Spike. "President Sullivan is not to be disturbed this morning."

"Sheesh." Mike shrugged. He was used to Spike being strict about rules. But it was pretty unusual for Mike not to know what Sulley was up to.

Mike headed to the locker room. He was just putting on his sweatband when Sulley suddenly rushed in.

"Hey, pal!" Mike said happily. "You ready to hit the gym?"

"Sorry, buddy, I've got to run," Sulley called. He grabbed a bottle from his locker and raced out the door.

Another Laugh Collector named Fungus was standing nearby. "I thought you two were best friends," he said.

"We *are* best friends," said Mike firmly. "I'm sure he's just busy right now." Still, Mike couldn't help feeling a little hurt.

Mike went into the gym. It was packed. There were monsters using weights, monsters riding exercise bikes, and even monsters lining up for Beastly Hula Dancing class.

Mike headed over to the two treadmills that he and Sulley always used. But when he got closer, he stopped dead in his tracks. Sulley was running on the treadmill, chatting with another monster!

What's going on here? Mike wondered.

As Mike stood there, the doors opened for the Beastly Hula Dancing class. He got caught in the mad rush to get inside.

"Excuse me," Mike said to the teacher, "but I'm not supposed to be in this class."

"Don't be silly!" she said. "Everyone is welcome!"

Hula dancing was a lot harder than it looked! By the time the class ended, Mike was completely exhausted. And Sulley was nowhere to be found.

By the lockers, Mike bumped into George Sanderson.

"I'm not sure I should tell you," George said nervously, "but I overheard Sulley say something strange. He was just in here with a monster I've never seen before. And Sulley told the new guy that he was going to be your replacement."

"He said *what?*" cried Mike.

George nodded. "I heard him say, 'You're the perfect monster to take over for Mike.'"

Mike couldn't believe it! How could Sulley replace him? Mike looked for Sulley in his office and on the Laugh Floor. But he was nowhere to be found.

Later, when Mike walked into the cafeteria for lunch, he glanced over at the table that he and Sulley usually shared. And there was Sulley, just finishing lunch with the new monster!

Mike stomped over to the table. He was so determined, he didn't notice that someone had spilled a huge bowl of red slime gelatin all over the floor.

"*Whoooooaaaaaa!*" yelled Mike as he slid across the cafeteria, his arms in the air. He crashed into a chair, flipped in the air, and landed on the dessert table!

There was a moment of shocked silence. Then everyone began laughing and cheering. Because Mike was so good at getting laughs, they thought he had done it on purpose!

"Bravo, Mike!" someone yelled.

By the time Mike had wiped the frosting off himself, Sulley was long gone.

Mike went to find Sulley to figure out what was going on once and for all.

He raced out of the cafeteria and caught sight of a long blue tail disappearing into the elevator. Aha! Mike thought. He ran down the hall. Just as the elevator doors were about to shut, he stuck his hand between them.

"Who do you think you are, you big furball?!" he cried.

The elevator doors slid open. And there stood another Laugh Collector who worked at Monsters, Inc.

"Aw, Mike," he sniffled. "Why do you have to be mean? I don't even have fur!"

Mike sighed. "Sorry, buddy. I didn't mean to yell. I thought you were someone else." Mike got in the elevator. It had been the worst day ever. And he still hadn't found Sulley.

Just as the elevator doors opened, Mike spotted a sign on a nearby door. Sulley was going to be there at four o'clock.

That's it! thought Mike. I'll just wait here for him. It's the only way to find out why I am being replaced.

Mike went in and sat down in one of the comfy chairs.

He had been so worked up all morning, he hadn't realized how tired he was. Within minutes, he slid off the chair and fell asleep under the table.

Zzzzzzzzz.

When Mike woke up, he was totally confused. He heard voices and laughter. He peeked out from under the tablecloth. It was a party!

Sulley was on the other side of the room. Behind him, Mike saw a sign that looked like it read: GOOD LUCK, MIKE! He couldn't believe it. He was at his own going-away party. He *was* being replaced!

Mike stormed across the room and stood in front of Sulley.

"Hey, Mike!" said Sulley. "Where have you been all day? There's someone I want you to meet."

"Now you listen to me, James P. Sullivan," Mike said angrily. "You are an awful . . ."

Just then, Sulley moved, and Mike was able to read the whole sign. It said: GOOD LUCK, SPIKE!

Mike stared. This wasn't a going-away party for him. It was for Sulley's assistant, Spike!

George Sanderson was nearby sipping punch. "Sorry, Mike." He shrugged. "Sulley came to the Laugh Floor after lunch to tell us about Spike's replacement and the party. My mistake!"

"Spike is moving to Slimeville. His cousin Spike J.—you know, from the Laugh Floor, has a place there," Sulley said. "So I hired a new assistant. I'd like you to meet Grunt. I've been showing him around. But no tour of Monsters, Inc. is complete without meeting our best Laugh Collector and my best friend, Mike Wazowski."

Sulley smiled at Mike. "Now what were you about to say?"

Mike thought fast. "Um . . . I was about to say that you are an awfully great boss—and an even better friend."

"Thanks, little buddy," Sulley said.

"It's a pleasure to meet you, Mr. Wazowski," said Grunt.

"Actually," said Mike, grinning, "the pleasure is all mine."

DISNEY·PIXAR
MONSTERS, INC.
Gettin' Groovy

One night, Mike Wazowski and his best friend, Sulley, were headed home after work. As they walked through Monstropolis, they saw a large banner.

"'Join us for the first-ever Monster Dance Talent Show,'" Sulley read aloud. "'This Saturday.'"

Mike squinted his eye. "Saturday?" He clapped his hands. "All right! This will be fun!"

"Um, Mike," Sulley said, "you realize that being in the talent show means you'll have to . . ." He trailed off. Sulley wasn't sure if his best buddy knew how to dance.

"Have to what?" Mike asked impatiently. "Sulley, what are you trying to say?"

"Well, you'll have to dance," Sulley said.

Mike twirled around and put out his hands in a "ta-da" pose. "That's just what I'm going to do." He grinned. "Dance away with the grand prize!"

"Googly Bear, wait up!"
Mike's girlfriend, Celia,
called as she ran toward
them. "I have fantastic
news. I'm going to do
a tap routine at the
talent show."

"Oh, yeah," Mike
said as Celia showed
them one of her tap
moves. "Monstropolis's
best dance teacher *has* to perform."

Celia taught tap dancing twice a week at Monster Studios. All
of her students loved her.

"I can't wait to see you," Mike continued. "And wait until you
see *me* onstage!"

"But Googly Bear, do you know how to dance?" Celia asked.

"Of course I do!" Mike said. "I boogie all the time!" He wiggled his hips to prove it.

"I think what Celia is trying to say, buddy," said Sulley, "is that you need to know a specific type of dance to be in the show."

"Don't worry," Mike told them. "I've got a plan."

Sulley raised an eyebrow. "A plan?"

"I'm going to take lessons this week at Monster Studios. And Sulley, you're going to join me!"

Sulley wasn't sure about Mike's plan. He found himself at the dance studio the next day anyway.

"I thought we'd start with ballet first," Celia said. She gave them tights and slippers. Then they went to a ballet classroom.

"Just follow the teacher," she whispered.

Mike groaned as he bent his knees. "These tights are so . . . uhhh . . . tight!"

"Try to keep up, buddy," Sulley said.

The teacher clapped her hands. "Are you ready, class? First, we jeté. Then we leap."

Mike and Sulley looked at each other. They didn't know how to jeté. But they sure could leap.

They took a running start and leaped across the room. But they had run so fast that they couldn't stop! *Crash!* They went right though the wall. Tutus flew everywhere. And the wall had a Sulley-shaped hole in it.

"Well, ballet is definitely out," Celia said. "Let's try tap." She pointed to a rack with shiny shoes. "Put these on, and we'll get started."

"This is great!" Mike exclaimed. He stood up, took two steps, and then slid across the floor. *"Whooooaa!"*

"Careful, Googly Bear!" Celia cried.

Sulley tapped his foot. "Hey, I've got rhythm!"

"And I've got the slips!" Mike said, falling again.

272

Celia took a deep breath. "Well, there's a hip-hop class going on down the hall," she said. "Maybe that will work."

Mike and Sulley put on caps and high-top sneakers. They started moving to the booming music.

When everyone spun to the left, Mike spun right. If the other monsters' arms were up, Mike's were down. He finished with a backflip . . . and landed on his back! *Whap!*

"There are so many kinds of dances," Mike said as they sat down on a bench in the hall.

"And so many kinds of shoes," Sulley added. He rubbed his sore, furry feet.

"I've got to learn one for the contest," Mike said glumly. "But none of them feels right."

Sulley and Celia both nodded. They wanted to help their friend, but they weren't sure how.

Just then, they heard loud music down the hall. Colored lights flashed through an open classroom door.

"What class is that?" Mike asked. He swayed to the beat of the music. "I love that song!"

Mike and Sulley peered into the room. It was disco class. A white suit and platform shoes were by the door.

"And this outfit is just my style!" he said as he put it on. "Let's go boogie!"

"I think he's found his dance," Sulley said as he watched his friend. "It's disco! And he's got some moves."

"How do I look?" Mike asked his friends as he spun.

Celia grinned. "You're a dancing fiend!" she said.

Mike rolled his hands up and down.

"Oh, I knew I had the moves. Plus, this is my kind of music." He pretended to hold a microphone in his hand. "Oogie, woogie, scoogie. Do the monster boogie!"

For the next week, Mike and Sulley went to Monster Studios every day to practice. "Sulley, you have rhythm," Celia said as she watched him tap dance one afternoon.

"Maybe you can dance together?" Mike suggested. "Double the tapping fun!"

"That's a great idea!" Celia exclaimed. "Sulley, would you be my partner in the talent show?"

"Gee, Celia," Sulley said. "I'd be honored."

"All right!" exclaimed Mike. "This Saturday's show is going to be the best show ever!"

Soon Saturday came. The theater was packed with monsters.

As the lights dimmed, a three-eyed ballerina took the stage. She began dancing a piece from *Swamp Lake*. Her tutu was made of long, colorful feathers that fanned out when she twirled.

Mike peeked through the curtain to watch. "Wow," he said. "She's really good." He looked at his friends. "Are you guys ready?" he whispered. "You're up next!"

After the ballerina was done, Sulley and Celia stepped out. They were wearing matching top hats, sequined vests, and bow ties.

The jazz song "Screaming for You" began playing. Celia and Sulley tapped out the rhythm in their shiny black shoes. *Click, clack, clickety-clack!*

Sulley tossed his hat in the air and caught it on his cane while Celia finished with a spin. The audience loved them!

As his friends bowed, Mike knew it was his turn. He walked to center stage and closed his eye. A spotlight focused on him, and the music started.

First he bounced his knee. Then he bobbed his head. Suddenly, "Do the Monster Boogie!" came on and a giant disco ball lit up.

Mike struck a pose. The audience went wild! They clapped along to the music and cheered him on.

Mike grinned. He turned, he kicked, he shuffled his feet, and he rolled his arms. He was having a great time!

Everyone wanted to join in. "Come on, everyone!" Mike said. "Get up and dance!"

Soon, all the monsters in the theater were lined up in the aisles, clapping and grooving to the music.

It was a giant disco party! The talent show had never been so much fun.

Mike waved for Celia and Sulley to join him onstage. He wanted to share this moment with his friends. He spun Celia around and ended with a grand dip. The crowd went wild!

The Monster Dance Talent Show had been a huge success. The three-eyed ballerina took the top prize. But all of Mike's friends said he was the most enthusiastic dancer they had ever seen. And to him, that was just groovy!

DISNEY·PIXAR

MONSTERS, INC.

What I Did on My Summer Vacation

One night, Mike was visiting Boo, the girl who had made friends with him and Sulley when she'd accidentally gone through her closet door and ended up at Monsters, Inc. They'd had to hide her then. Now everything was different. Monsters, Inc. used laughter for energy instead of screams. So Mike visited Boo and made her giggle whenever he could.

But this time, Boo wasn't laughing at Mike's tricks. "Is something wrong, Boo?" Mike asked.

Boo pointed to some pictures of her school and of classmates who were holding up photos.

"School starts!" Boo said. "No photos!"

285

Luckily, Mike quickly figured out what Boo meant. School was about to begin, and she wanted to tell her class what she'd done over vacation. But she hadn't really gone anywhere that summer.

"Why don't you come to Monsters, Inc. with me?" Mike suggested. "We'll surprise Sulley."

Boo jumped up excitedly. "Yay!"

Boo and Mike went to Monsters, Inc. by stepping through Boo's closet door.

"Follow me," said Mike. "I have something you can borrow."

Mike took an old camera from on top of a supply closet. "Let's see if it still works," he said.

"EEP!" he cried when Boo snapped his picture.

Boo laughed so hard that the lights flickered.

"Yup, I guess it works," said Mike. "You can use it to take pictures of this trip."

Then Mike led Boo to the Laugh Floor.

"Oh, Sulleeey!" he called out to his blue, furry friend. "I have a surprise for you."

"Kitty!" Boo exclaimed.

Sulley was surprised. He wrapped her in a big hug.

Everyone on the Laugh Floor was excited to see Boo.
Many of the monsters showed off their new tricks. Boo
took lots of pictures.

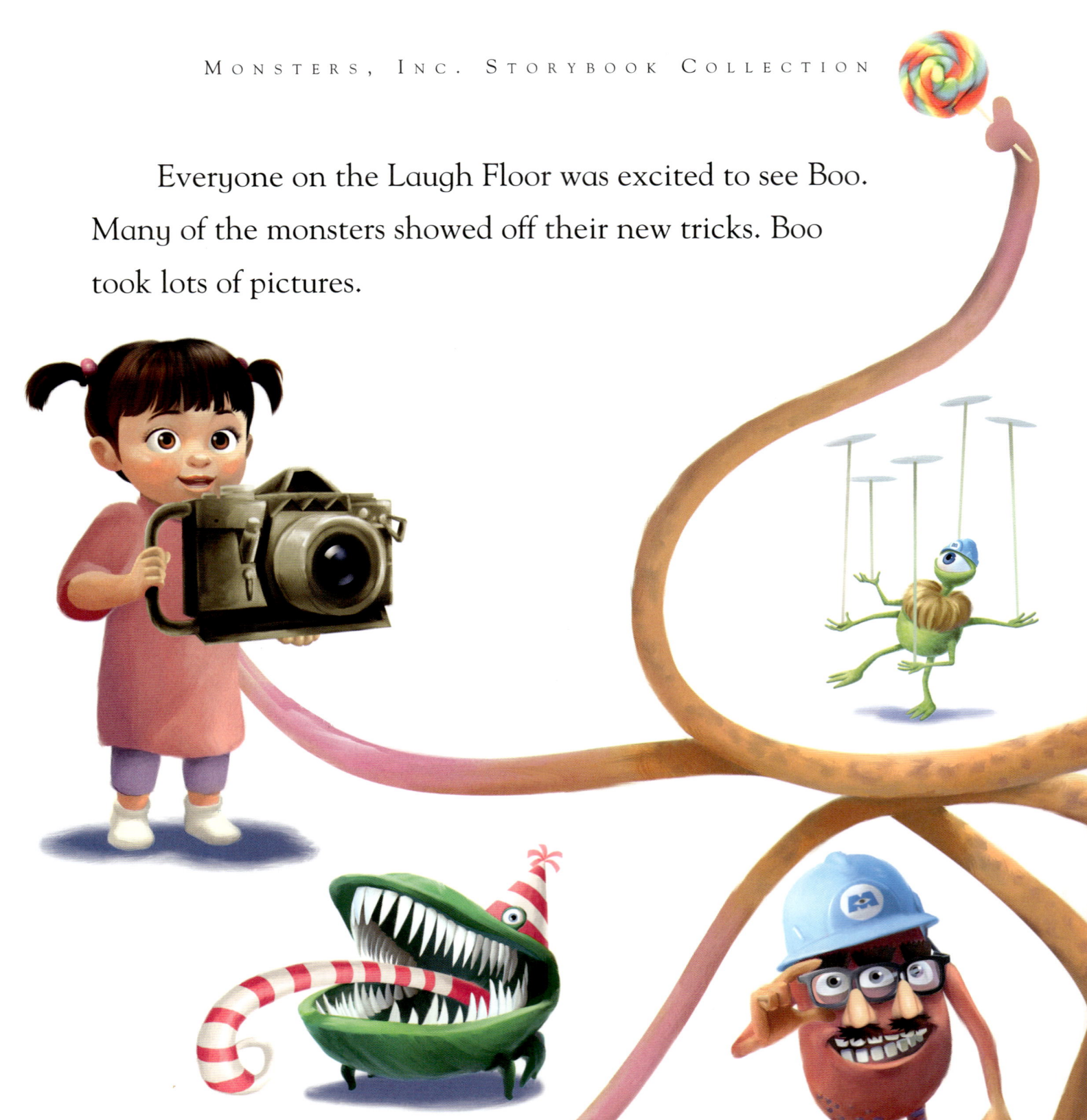

All night long, Boo, Mike, and Sulley raced from one place to another. Boo had a party, went to a water park, and even played on the beach! Mike wanted to make sure she had lots of pictures so it would be like she had had a whole summer vacation in just one night.

By the end of the visit, Boo had taken tons of photos. She and Mike were trying to decide which were the best ones to bring to school.

Sulley frowned. "School? What do you mean 'school'? Boo can't take these picture to the human world. Then it won't be a secret."

Boo was disappointed. "Please, Kitty?" she said.

"Okay," Sulley said finally. "I'll let you take back one photo. But I get to pick it."

Mike grinned, and Boo cheered.

The teacher gasped. "That looks like Bigfoot!"

Boo's classmates gasped.

Boo giggled. The picture was very blurry. It was hard to tell what it even was. "Not Bigfoot. That's Kitty!"

Sulley had made sure humans wouldn't find out about monsters from Boo! But even though no one believed her, Boo would always remember her wonderful vacation!

At school the next day, Boo told her class all about her special adventure.

Her classmates didn't believe her.

Her teacher didn't believe her.

So Boo pulled out the picture. . . .